The Holiday Bride
Paperback Copyright © 2022 Lorhainne Ekelund
Editor: Talia Leduc

All rights reserved.
ISBN-13: 978-1998775101

Give feedback on the book at:
lorhainneeckhart@hotmail.com

Twitter: @LEckhart
Facebook: AuthorLorhainneEckhart

Printed in the U.S.A

The Holiday Bride

THE WILDE BROTHERS

LORHAINNE ECKHART

The Wilde Brothers

Come and meet the Wilde Brothers of Idaho. Joe, Logan, Ben, Samuel, and Jake. You'll love the western flair and hot men and strong women in this romantic family saga.

The One
The Honeymoon
Friendly Fire
A Matter of Trust
The Reckoning
Traded
Unforgiven
The Holiday Bride

All Trinity Cooper Wilde wanted was a quiet Christmas alone with her baby, a baby no one knows about but her twin sister, Dawn.*

Dawn has warned Trinity that she needs to come clean and tell everyone about the baby, including the father, Garrett Franke, their former neighbor, whom Trinity has hated since tenth grade—with the exception of one night last year, a mistake.

Her family is starting to wonder why she hasn't come home to visit in over six months, and Trinity knows time is running out. She plans to tell everyone, but she gets happily stuck in an unexpected snowstorm in her tiny cabin, located outside a small Idaho town.

Deputy Garrett Franke still can't get Trinity out of his mind, especially considering he works side by side with her dad, Sheriff Logan Wilde. When Dawn unexpectedly pulls him aside one day, he allows her to convince him to drive out to a remote cabin in the middle of a snowstorm to check on her sister, whom no one has heard from since the storm hit.

That's the thing about snowstorms: You never know who'll show up at your door, and a baby isn't the kind of secret that can stay that way for long.

CHAPTER
One

Why was it that her phone always rang exactly when the baby went down?

Trinity raced across her cabin in her flannel pajamas and socks. Her cell phone, which she had forgotten to mute, was lit up on the butcher-block counter in the tiny kitchen, ringing like a fire alarm.

"Ah, shit!" she muttered and winced as she stubbed her toe on the leg of a stool she hadn't pushed in. She landed on the phone before it could ring a third time. "Hello?" she whispered, putting all the pissed-off tone she could muster into the word. She stared at the open door to the only bedroom, through which she could just make out the crib. Time stood still as she waited for the cry.

"Whoa, geez, did I wake you?"

It was Dawn, her sister.

Trinity pressed her hand to her chest, over the swell of her breasts, feeling grungy after having opted for sleep instead of a shower. In her pajamas, she felt the chill of the cabin. She needed to get more wood for the fire, too, considering she didn't think it was still going.

"Just got the baby down, and the phone just about woke her," she said. "I was considering a shower even though I'd love nothing more than to grab a few more hours." She groaned and caught a whiff of something off, then lifted her arm and realized it was her. Yup, the shower had now moved up the list of necessities.

"Sleep?" said Dawn. "What the fuck, Trinity? You were supposed to be on the road, remember, for Christmas at Mom and Dad's? You are not going to chicken out! Tell me you're going to show up, please, because if you don't, Mom and Dad are likely to drive up, and then they'll know I've been lying to them. Mom told me just yesterday you were sounding unusually tired, and here's me, having to cover your butt yet again. I said it was likely a deadline, because you've picked up a lot of new clients and are trying to accomplish the impossible, and you were probably pulling an all-nighter again. I swear I can feel my nose grow. I seriously wonder if she can tell I'm lying. Good thing Dad wasn't there, because he'd have known for sure…"

Trinity held the phone away from her ear, still not missing the rest of her sister's rant. Boy, Dawn could get mad when she wanted to, and Trinity knew that the little secret she'd been keeping from everyone except her sister had only dug her into a hole she didn't think she could get out of.

Avoidance was just something she'd become really good at.

"I'm coming," she said. "I told you I would. I was just up most of the night with the baby, and I'm so damn tired I can feel it in my bones. I'm sure you don't want me driving on these roads with a baby, ready to fall asleep." She knew she was spreading it on thick, but at the same time, nervousness had been nipping at her butt again. If she could just find an excuse someone would buy, she'd be able to get out of going home to her parents' place for Christmas. "So stop panicking. I promised I would come and face the music."

Right, the music—which was her parents and the fact that she had a baby only her sister knew about. Like, who did that?

In fact, the baby's father was the real issue: Garrett Franke, her dad's deputy, whom she'd hated since the tenth grade. What had she been thinking? He was tall and dark haired, and she was a sucker for his drawl and smile.

A momentary lapse. She'd not spoken to him once since their night together.

"Look, if you're that tired, I can come and get you," Dawn said. "Even better, how about Mom or Dad—or, better yet, both? Then you can explain about the baby before you see everyone, and I won't have to be there when they realize I've been lying to them for nine months! And while we're at it, Trinity, you need to pick a name for the baby. I gave you my ideas already, so just pick one and go with it."

Dawn's names were all from the list of the top forty in the country—Amelia, Joy, Iris, Kennedy…as if one of them would fit. Trinity strode over to the sink and reached for a glass, then turned on the tap and filled it with water. On the table sat her open laptop and notes from her current client's website design, which was only in the beginning stages. Right, something else she still needed to do. She could finish if only she didn't have to leave her cabin.

There it was again, that wistful longing for a Christmas alone with her baby. Why did the thought appeal to her like the perfect present?

"I told you I'm working on a name," Trinity said. "It has to be perfect."

"You're kidding, right? She's six weeks old already. Just pick one," Dawn said.

There it was, the constant nagging. Dawn just didn't get the fact that Trinity needed to take her time. She couldn't be pushed. As with learning to swim, she couldn't jump in the deep end of the pool; she needed to wade in carefully to make sure nothing could go wrong.

"Stop pushing, Dawn," she said. "I already told you I'll be there. You don't need to come and get me. I just need to shower and grab some coffee…" And pack up any clean clothes she could find, considering having a new baby meant no laundry was getting done.

She would be driving right into the lion's den, so to speak. She'd avoided Idaho Falls for just that reason. First, Garrett was there, and second, she knew when her parents found out about the baby, they would have a lot of questions she didn't want to answer. Her dad would likely sit her down and start in with his cop interrogation until he found out the real reason she had wanted no one to know.

"So you promise this time you're coming?" Dawn said.

What was it about being put on the spot that made her want to say no?

"Yes, even though I want nothing more than a Christmas alone with my baby without having to sit through Dad's interrogation or Mom's freak-out over the fact that I had a baby and didn't tell them. You said everyone's going to be there, right? All Dad's brothers, and Gram and Gramps and… That's a lot of people, and they're all going to be asking me the one thing I don't want anyone to know: who the father is. You know, maybe Christmas isn't the time for this."

"Don't you dare," Dawn said, and Trinity could feel the bite in her voice. Someone spoke in the background—she wasn't sure who—before Dawn lowered her voice and said in a loud whisper, "You pack up that baby right now, and figure out a name for her by the time you get here. You get in that four by four and drive, because if you don't, I will tell Mom and Dad…and then there's Garrett."

Trinity didn't miss the threat in her words. "Dawn, don't tell Garrett," she snapped. "You promised me you wouldn't say anything, and I'm holding you to it. I do not want him to know."

"Fine," Dawn replied. "I know what you said, but you can't keep the baby a secret forever. You know that, and I know that. I can't believe I let you talk me into saying nothing. A baby is a really big deal, and the thing about babies is that you can't keep them a secret forever. You know it's not going to take anyone, especially Garrett, too long to figure out from the timeframe that the baby is his. You'd best take the bull by the horns and come clean. He has a right to know, Trinity, no matter what. And then there're Mom and Dad. You know they won't let it go."

She squeezed the phone, furious at her sister, just as she heard the first cry and knew her shower was now going to have to wait. "Fine, but I'm not telling Garrett," she said. "The baby's awake now. I have to go…"

She could hear her sister still talking as she disconnected the phone, furious at the guilt that she didn't want to feel. After all, Garrett was her dad's deputy, and hadn't she heard that he was already hooking up with a friend of Dawn's now?

As she took in her quiet cabin, she wanted nothing more than to have a few more hours of peace and quiet alone with her baby before all hell broke loose and she had to face her mom and dad's inquisition. Worse, she was dreading the minute her dad found out his deputy was in fact the baby's father.

CHAPTER

Two

"Wow, it's really coming down out there," Dawn said as she dropped into the sheriff's office. "Cars are spinning out of control, and it's practically white-out conditions. Did you get all your Christmas shopping done?"

Something about her was more quirky than usual today. Actually, scratch that. This was the third time Garrett had noticed her coming in, so he took a closer look as she pulled off her gloves and coat and brushed the snow from her short dark hair. Her striking green eyes weren't filled with the usual mischief. Something was off.

"Sure," he replied and lifted his hand to show the Santa mug he was holding, which held stale coffee. It was his gift from the office exchange, from the matronly office manager, Rose. He had drawn the sheriff's name, and he still wasn't sure Logan had appreciated the book of random potty jokes, the first thing he'd seen in the dollar store—though Rose had made it clear that ten dollars was the limit and they would have to be creative. "You looking for your dad? Because he's out on a call and asked me to hold down the office. Not sure how long he'll be, Dawn."

She just made a face and shrugged. "No, I'm not here to see my dad. Thought I'd stop in and bug you, is all."

This was odd. He couldn't help thinking she was up to something. "In the middle of a snowstorm?" he said, doing his best not to laugh. As she leaned against his desk, he could see she didn't appreciate being called out. There was just something about her today that went beyond the usual Dawn weirdness.

The fax dinged and started spitting out paper, and he found himself taking in the way Dawn lingered as he walked over to it. Was she flirting? No, but she definitely wanted something. He said nothing.

"So what are you and Lori doing for Christmas, again?" she said.

He reached for the papers, seeing the notes from the sheriff a county over, an arrest report and a summary of road conditions. The unexpected storm wasn't really unexpected, considering snow and white-out conditions were the norm every winter. He was prepared for a long Christmas of calls, likely all of them vehicle-related, because it seemed everyone forgot how to drive as soon as the first snowflake fell.

He tossed Dawn a sideways glance. Something about her smile seemed off, something he couldn't put his finger on. She was up to something. Maybe.

"Nothing," he replied. "I'm working over Christmas. Your dad needs someone to man the phones and the office, and that's me. I drew the short straw. That's the single life."

He and Lori were on the back burner, taking a break, considering she had suddenly wanted to change their casual relationship into a commitment, and that kind of said everything about where their relationship was going. At the same time, he wasn't about to share anything from his personal life with Dawn, considering it would likely all go right to his boss, her dad.

He'd already made the mistake of mixing business with pleasure once—with Trinity.

"Hmm," was all she said, and he took another second to look down at her. She was cute, attractive, slim, and the spitting image of her sister. He had to look away.

"So what's going on, Dawn? You want something?" he said as he walked the papers over to Rose's empty desk. Seeing nothing urgent, he rested them in her inbox for her to deal with.

"Just wanted to talk to you and catch up, is all," she said. "We haven't done that in quite a while. I only see you when I drop in to see Dad or when you're out on patrol or something. I kind of miss that lopsided smile and all that handsomeness."

He dragged his gaze back over to her, and she flashed him another one of her cute smiles. She was wearing blue jeans, and her hiking boots were caked in snow.

"You hitting on me there, Dawn?"

The shock in her expression was priceless. "What? No!" She actually reached out and swatted his arm, and he was at least glad he had settled that issue. He blew out a breath of relief. "You think I want to be added to the list of ladies you can't or won't commit to? Seriously, Garrett, you may be a hot, confident, arrogant cop, and those pretty-boy features of yours may have all the women you date thinking that they can get their hooks into you and find a way to settle you down, but I'm not one of them. Besides, aren't you and Lori still an item?" She lifted her hands, and he took her in. She could be amusing at times, but something about the way she had said it and the way she kept prying had him trying to figure out what was really up with her.

"Lori and I aren't serious," he said. "Everyone knows that. So if this isn't you hitting on me, then what gives, Dawn? And aren't you dating that rich dude again, Dwayne Do-gooder or whatever the hell his name is?"

She was unimpressed. Then again, he recalled that her dad, the sheriff, had even asked him to run a background check on the guy. "You know his name is Hadley Reynolds," Dawn said, "and we're kind of taking a break." She shrugged and slapped her gloves together, and he wasn't sure what to make of her expression. "He's in Germany right now, handling some crisis, and we decided to cool things down. Considering he hops on a plane every time some disaster happens, it makes it kind of difficult to build a relationship. More often than not, we're in opposite time zones. When I call him, he's asleep, and then he calls me back and it's the middle of the night."

She forced one of those uncomfortable smiles to her face again, and this time he really looked at the way she was standing, her expression. Her casual dismissal didn't seem all that convincing, and she was now gripping the cell phone she had pulled from her coat pocket, the second time she'd looked at it.

"Okay, spill," Garrett said. "Something's up, and I hardly think you're here just to chat. What's really going on? And no more bullshit." He tacked the snow report and notice of a road closure on the interstate up on the bulletin board and walked back over to his desk.

Dawn squeezed her phone and then lifted her hands. "Fine. Look, Trinity was supposed to be on her way. She's coming home for Christmas and should be here by now, but I haven't heard from her. I've been calling her cell phone, and now it says she can't be reached, which likely means the cell towers are down. If I didn't make it clear, the snow is really coming down…" She bit her lip, and he had a sinking feeling he wasn't going to like this.

He said nothing as he stared down at her. Yeah, Trinity and him were like oil and water, not something he wanted to talk about. Nor did he want to relive their one night together, which never should have happened. What about sleeping with his boss's daughter had he thought was a good idea at the time? All her sass and back talk, her smart mouth… He pulled in a breath and forced her sweet, sexy image from his mind once again. *Nope, not going to happen!*

"And why aren't you talking to your dad about this?" Garrett said. "Just FYI, she probably took a look at the snow and realized the smart thing to do was stay put. At least one of you two has some sense."

Dawn grabbed his arm, her entire demeanor switching from playful to desperate. "Look, Garrett, seriously, as you said, my dad is out on a call. I'm worried. I mean, I could go looking for her, but the road conditions are questionable, and if I head up the mountain where she insisted on buying that damn cabin, I'll likely end up in a ditch, and then my dad will wonder where I am, considering I promised my mom I'd help her with baking and getting the house ready for the holidays…"

He knew his mouth was open. He lifted his gaze to the ceiling as she went on and on, knowing Logan would be furious that Garrett had suggested Dawn handle this when he should go himself. At the same time, why wasn't his boss already all over this? After all, Trinity was his daughter.

"Stop!" Garrett snapped. "Give me your sister's number, and I'll call her. If she doesn't answer, then I'll go up there and see that she's fine. At least she had enough sense to stay put."

Dawn squealed and threw her arms around him, reaching up over his shoulders and bouncing up and down. Then she jumped back, her expression suddenly excited—no, overjoyed. Of course, he couldn't help but smile.

"That's great," she said. "I'll write down her number for you, but then you hop right into your truck and drive up to where she lives." She reached for a pen and paper on his desk and gestured to him. "Oh, and don't take no for an answer from her if she's there. Just pack her up and bring her here. Don't leave her in the cabin, because it's Christmas, and she promised everyone she'd be here."

He just stared down at Dawn as she scribbled out Trinity's phone number and address. He couldn't help thinking this was what she'd planned before walking through the door. What was it with women? Either they were trying to get a ring on his finger, or they were trying to work some angle and make him think it was his idea.

It was no wonder he was still single—and happily so. Yeah, he definitely had no plans to get tied up in that trap at any time in the foreseeable future.

Dawn lifted her hand in a wave as she skipped out of the office, and Garrett just shook his head and folded up the paper.

"Women," he muttered under his breath.

CHAPTER
Three

Trinity could hear the baby crying inside the cabin as she finished brushing the snow off her Jeep, which she'd packed up with luggage. She had been warming up the car for the past twenty minutes, and it was now dark, late afternoon. She'd fallen asleep again after feeding her baby, knowing she should've been on the road hours ago.

The snow was really coming down now, and the wind seemed to have come out of nowhere, creating almost white-out conditions. She now couldn't even see the break in the trees at the end of the narrow driveway only a hundred feet from her cabin. To make matters worse, she knew the temperature had dropped to the twenties, not the kind of weather she wanted to go anywhere in.

"Coming, baby girl…" she called out as she tossed the snow brush to the floor of the back seat, still feeling how cold the vehicle was. The conditions were far from ideal for a newborn.

She shut the door and stepped through knee-high snow back to the front steps and into the semi-warm cabin, where she knocked the snow off her boots, still kicking herself for falling asleep for three hours.

There was something about having a newborn baby that no one could have prepared her for. There were the midnight, three a.m., and six a.m. feedings, then checking and double-checking to make sure her baby was still breathing. It was a fear she couldn't explain to anyone, because they'd likely think she was crazy.

And she still hadn't figured out a name for the baby that was unlike the names everyone else had— Jane, Karen, Gina.

She slipped off her coat and dumped it on the older tweed sofa with its orange and brown crocheted blanket, tossed in a heap. The fire had gone out long ago, and she hurried to the crib, taking in how tiny her baby was. She was wearing a mint-colored sleeper Dawn had given her and a matching hat, and she had kicked the blanket off and was waving her tiny fists in the air.

"Shh, baby…" Trinity lifted her and felt the dampness in her diaper. She carried her over to the window, seeing her Jeep still running and covered once again with snow, feeling the stress and angst and worry as each second ticked by, dreading the minute she would face her mom and dad and tell them she'd been lying to them from the moment she'd found out she was pregnant.

What was it about digging herself into a hole and

avoiding something? The more time passed, the more excuses she seemed to pile on. Why had it seemed like a good idea to keep her baby a secret?

She took in her baby, who was only six weeks old, and the car seat by the door, wishing for a miracle that would keep her home another day, just one more day, or better yet, until after Christmas.

"What do you think?" she said. "I'll start the fire, and we can stay home and make our excuses. We'll say it's just too bad out there, that the snow is too heavy. I'll call Mom and Dad…but you'd like to meet your grandparents, wouldn't you?"

Her baby's eyes were open, and she was working her tiny fist into her mouth, sucking away. Just her and her baby and no one to tell her what to do, how to think, how to feel… But she knew time was up with her sister. Dawn would blow a gasket, and there was no way Trinity would get away with not showing up.

She patted her baby's bottom. "And I need to figure out the perfect name for you. Skye… What do you think? I've always loved that name." She took in her daughter. "Wishful thinking. Guess it's now or never. Come, I'll get you changed, and then we'd better go."

Trinity quickly changed and bundled up the baby before securing her in the baby carrier, all the while thinking of names. She buckled her in back and put a quilt over her. The snow was really coming down now.

"How about Olivia, after my grandma? Hmm, no. You don't look like an Olivia, either." She patted her baby, hoping she stayed quiet for the hour it would take to drive into Idaho Falls, through town, and to her parents' place.

She shut the door and climbed behind the wheel, turning on the wiper to clear the windshield of all the fresh snow, and put the Jeep in reverse. When she backed up, she heard the wheels whir and slip in, and she flicked on her lights, seeing snow thick in the rearview mirror. She drove from memory only, knowing where the gravel driveway was, and made it another foot before she was stuck and her tires started spinning.

"Oh, shit…" She tapped the wheel and then threw it in reverse again, glancing to her baby but seeing only the back of the car seat. She pressed the gas, hearing the whir of the engine, the tires spinning and the Jeep going nowhere. When she gave it more gas, it shifted forward, and she felt it give just a bit before it sank deeper into the snow, the wheels spinning. She was completely stuck.

Nothing like realizing her wish was coming true at the wrong time. She had spent a long while away from her family, and how would they take this latest news of her not coming once again? Not well, she was positive.

She climbed out of the Jeep into snow that was so deep that it filled her boots immediately, and a quick look at the front end and the buried wheels told her there was no way she was getting out. It looked as if she had parked in a snowdrift, but at least they were only about twenty feet from the front of her cabin.

She lifted her daughter from the back seat and hefted her through the snow, back inside the darkened cabin. When she flicked the switch for the light, she was glad it turned on, because the only thing that would make this worse would be to lose power.

Then she caught the flicker of headlights and the sound of a vehicle, and she turned in the open door, seeing a truck with a snow-shovel blade in front of it, clearing the way around her Jeep.

As she watched, her stomach pitched. The sheriff's logo was visible on the side door, and her alarm bells went off. It had to be her dad! She felt like a teenager again, and her mind went blank as to how she would explain this, her baby.

She slammed the door to the cabin, feeling panic lick at the back of her throat as she stared down at her baby, who appeared sound asleep now. Then she did the one thing she'd never expected she'd do: She flicked off the lights, stepped outside, and pulled the door closed behind her.

The lights of the truck were in her face, blinding her, and the door was open on the driver's side. Time had suddenly run out, and she pasted a smile to her face as she took in the tall man in a heavy coat and hat stepping around the vehicle.

Then her world tilted.

Garrett Franke walked toward her, tall and rugged, and for a second, she had to remind herself to breathe.

Garrett couldn't believe he'd let Dawn work him the way she had. What was it with women and their ability to get him to do exactly what they wanted? Now here he was, driving up the mountain to where Trinity lived in a quaint cabin, as her mom, Julia, had put it. Logan had only shaken his head and muttered when she said that. The place was secluded and ridiculous.

He worked the blade on the front of the truck to clear the snow on the barely passable road. His wipers were going a mile a minute, and he had to use his GPS to find the cabin, down a driveway that wasn't marked. He drove in, seeing her Jeep parked at an odd angle, the door open. Yeah, she was definitely stuck and wasn't going anywhere. As he pulled up to the cabin, he saw it from both Julia's and Logan's views.

Then Trinity stepped out, flicked the lights off, and pulled the door closed behind her. Like, what the fuck? He parked the truck but left it running as he stepped out, the headlights on. He knew they were blinding her, but he took his time, taking in her rusty bomber jacket, cream hat and scarf, and blue jeans tucked into boots covered in snow up to her knees.

He inhaled as he stepped out and around the open door, then gave it a shove closed and started around the front of his truck to the step. Her hand was up, likely from the lights, trying to make him out. With her plump cheeks and full lips, she may have resembled Dawn, but there was nothing the same about her and her sister.

"You're stuck," he spat out and stopped at the first of the three steps up to her wooden porch, with its two small windows and a chair just outside the door. He could see wood stacked in a box and then made himself look back over to Trinity. She stood in shock —no, alarm, maybe, as her mouth opened and nothing came out.

Then he looked at the closed door behind her and listened to his truck, which was still running. The noise of the engine was welcome. "Your sister insisted I come up here and check on you. She's been calling your cell over and over," he said. "So have I, but it seems the cell towers are down. No service up here. Not surprising, considering this."

It was a bad time of year, too. He couldn't even explain the panic he'd felt when he'd called and heard the automated beeping. He took in the snow that was blowing in, with visibility approaching zero. "You're supposed to be at your mom and dad's, but I can see there's no way you're getting out. Lucky for you that I came up here."

The minute he said it, he watched the change in her expression. What was it about her face that it showed him exactly how she felt about him? She disliked—no, despised him. Yet he wondered if he'd ever get that night out of his head, the sex, the passion, how she'd responded to him. It hadn't just been sex; it had been a momentary lapse that shouldn't have felt so right.

He found himself smiling at her eyes, the same green as Dawn's but far different, as they seemed to flash with hate. Something about her just had him wanting to push all her buttons.

"Why are you here?" she said, and he didn't miss her ingratitude.

"Wow. 'Geez, Garrett, thanks for driving all the way out here to check on me and see if I'm okay,'" he said, dripping sarcasm. "'Thanks for going out of your way, risking your life on roads that shouldn't be driven on. I'm mighty appreciative.' I think that's what you meant to say."

She crossed her arms and glanced to the side. Something about the way she stood in front of that door told him she wasn't about to invite him in, so he dragged his gaze back to where her Jeep was, its back door wide open.

"Seriously?" she said. "Wow, still the same arrogant, full-of-yourself jerk. I'm fine, as you can see, snowed in but fine, so you can turn your ass around, climb back in your truck, and leave. Tell my sister she doesn't need to worry, and tell my mom and dad sorry about Christmas, but as you can see, I'm not getting out. I'm snowed in." She rested her hand on the door to the cabin, and he was sure she was about to walk back in and slam the door in his face. She was still the same stuck up, pole-up-her-ass bitch he remembered, so what the hell was wrong with him that he was still imagining her naked?

"Yeah, well, lucky for you that I'm here," he said. "Grab your things, throw them in the back of the truck, and climb in. I'll drive you to your parents' and drop you off, and then I can get back to work—and help those who really need help."

She was shaking her head, and he wasn't sure what to make of her expression as she lifted her hands in the air. He even thought she dropped the F-bomb under her breath. Her smart mouth had often told him straight where to go. He started walking to her Jeep.

"Hey, where are you going?" she called out, and he heard her jump off the porch and into the snow behind him. He turned to see her running the best she could, snow up to her knees.

"You left your door open," he said. "I'm shutting it. I presume your bags are inside. I'll grab them, toss them in my truck, and then we can get the hell out of here before I can't see anything. Come on, the more snow comes down out here, the worse the roads get."

She grabbed his arm and raced past him, nearly going face down in the snow. "No! Wait, I can shut my own door."

He took in how ridiculous she looked as she ran—no, hopped through the snow as fast as she could, and he stopped. "Fine, do it yourself. For Christ's sake, Trinity, I swear you could drive a sober man to start drinking. I'm just trying to help. You want to grab your own bags, be my guest, do it yourself, but grab them already, and let's go."

She was already walking back toward him, trudging through the snow, breathing heavy. "No, you go," she said. "I'm staying home. Just send my apologies to my parents…"

What the fuck? Yup, she was definitely not anything like Dawn, giving him the same attitude she'd always sent his way. So how, again, had they ended up in bed?

"You want me to talk to your parents for you? And, what, tell them you're snowed in, yet when I drove all the way up here to check on you, you decided to stay home, alone, at Christmas—and I just drove away and let you? What gives, Trinity? There's no way. Seriously, grab your stuff, and I'll drive you. Or is this about me? If it is, get the fuck over it, already, because I have, and I'm not fucking around on these roads in this weather. In case you don't see it, there's a fucking snowstorm right now, and I'm not driving all the way back to Idaho Falls to tell your dad you decided to skip Christmas and hole up here in the middle of nowhere. FYI, once I leave here, no one is likely to get in with this storm. If your dad doesn't kill me, it'll be by some sheer miracle, so get your damn bags or I will, and let's go." He gestured to his truck and rested his hands on his belt with his holstered gun, like he did when dealing with assholes to show that he was the one in charge.

But she just kept walking right past him, and he took her in. Something was so off, and he couldn't put his finger on it. Between Dawn and Trinity, there was just something about the Wilde girls that he swore could drive a man crazy, except they were polar opposites.

"No, no, no, Garrett," she said. "Not sure what the problem is, but you're not hearing me." She was on her porch again, stamping the snow off her boots, and she glanced to the door, her hand on the knob as if ready to go in and slam it shut behind her. "Go, I'm fine," she continued. "I'll call my family and tell them, and you'll be off the hook. Then you don't have to even mention to my dad that you came out here." She actually brushed her hands together, and he could see how cold she had to be. It was freezing out there, and he could see her breath. Even his fogged before him. "You can give yourself a pat on the back, too, or whatever it is that overinflated ego of yours needs. Tell yourself you did the 'good guy' thing and made sure I was alive and well. So go on, now."

She actually flicked her hand, and he could feel his irritation mounting. It had him rolling his shoulders, and he pulled his gaze away before he did something he shouldn't, like toss her over his shoulders, stick her in the back seat, and lock her in. He had to fight the urge to smile, as the thought appealed to him in ways he knew it shouldn't.

"Not sure who you think you're talking to, Trinity, but I asked you to get your things. You're beginning to piss me off. I'll give to the count of three, or else I'm going to toss you over my shoulder and into the back seat, and we'll just forget your things. Makes no difference to me one way or the other, but we're leaving, and I can assure you the last thing I want to do is sit here and argue with you."

The look on her face was priceless. She actually stepped back right against the door. "You wouldn't dare!" she said. Of course she wouldn't make it easy, so he took one of the steps up, barely cleared of snow, and then another. She wasn't smiling when he stood right in front of her, but she had to look up, as the top of her head barely passed his shoulders.

"I warned you, Trinity, I'm not messing around."

"Don't you dare put one hand on me..." she started, but he bent down and lifted her.

Her hands swatted at him, and he somehow tossed her over his shoulder. She squealed as he went down the steps, cussing and screaming and fighting like a wildcat. He gripped her flailing arms and somehow pulled open the back door of the truck to toss her in, then shut it behind her. She had to realize, being in the back of his truck now, she was automatically locked in.

Maybe he shouldn't have taken such enjoyment from the horror on her face as her hands pressed and pounded against the glass. He took a second to see her Jeep stuck off to the side in the snowbank, then over to her cabin, where the door was closed, and he yanked his toque down over his ears, trying to block out whatever the hell she was yelling and carrying on about.

One thing set Trinity apart from Dawn: She could be a pain in the ass when she wanted to be.

Right. This was going to be a long, painful ride down the mountain.

He'd just tossed her into the back of his truck, where he put criminals, and her baby was still in the cabin. She pounded on the side window with her fists, screaming his name over and over, but what did he do but ignore her? He climbed behind the wheel, and she couldn't even reach over the seat to grab him, because a wire mesh was separating them.

"Garrett, stop! Let me out right now. You can't do this. This is completely illegal. This is kidnapping. This is so…"

His arm was over the passenger seat as he backed up, flooring it, driving incredibly fast for the amount of snow there was, and she stared in horror at her cabin, where her tiny, innocent baby was inside, all alone. The agony that ripped at her heart was like nothing she'd ever experienced, and he was ignoring her. Her tears were streaming, and she could feel panic clawing as she fought to breathe.

"Stop!" she screamed. "My baby is inside! Go back, Garrett, please stop." She was having a hard time seeing him. He was blurry. The truck skidded and the brakes slammed, and she pulled her hands over her eyes, swiping at the tears.

"What?" was all he said.

She smacked the wire mesh, then pulled her hands over her wet face again and took in the way he was staring at her in horror, disbelief. She feared for a second he wouldn't believe her, and maybe that was why she was now doing that ugly-cry thing and gulping for breath.

Oh, this couldn't be happening. She kept swiping at her eyes, and something in his expression was unlike the amused arrogant asshole who had tossed her into the back seat.

"Trinity, what the fuck did you just say? A baby, for real—or are you fucking around again? Between you and your sister, the games that go on, I swear to God Almighty…"

"Damn you, Garrett! My baby is inside. Yes, I said 'baby.' Let me out of here right now!" She slammed the mesh again, then the side window and door, even though there was no way in hell she could get out.

He turned around, threw the truck in gear, and drove back up to the cabin, where he shoved it in park and turned off the engine before stepping out. She waited for him to open the back door, but instead he walked away, leaving her locked inside.

As he strode up the steps to her cabin, she

smacked the mesh again. "Garrett, you asshole! Let me out of here!"

But he didn't turn and gave no indication that he could hear her, and she watched in horror as he opened the door and flicked on the light. She knew there was no way of getting out until he decided to let her out. She hated being at his mercy this way. All she could do was stare at his back.

He turned his head and looked down, and she knew he had to be looking right at her baby—their baby. This was worse than she could have imagined, and she didn't have a clue what he was thinking as he turned back in the doorway. She wished she could have slugged him right then, as she curled her fingers, fighting the urge and wanting nothing more than to scream and yell at him and call him every name imaginable, then give him very direct instructions on the way to hell.

The door was still wide open, the light spilling out, as he strode down the steps and to the back door of the truck. He yanked it open. "Are you kidding me, Trinity? You have a baby?" he said.

As far as she was concerned, he had no right to be angry with her. She jumped out of the back and nearly landed in a bank of snow. If he hadn't reached out and grabbed her arm to right her, she swore she'd have gone face first. She yanked her arm away and forced herself not to look at him even though she could feel his gaze burning into her. All the while, she was telling herself, *He doesn't know, he doesn't know…*

"And you nearly drove away with me locked in the

back seat, leaving my baby alone in a storm. Who's the asshole, Garrett? You, that's who!"

She wasn't sure what he said behind her, but she thought he swore. She raced inside and took in her baby, sound asleep in her car seat on the floor, not having a clue what had almost happened. She knelt down, unfastened her, and lifted her out. The baby made that soft murmur she did when asleep, and Trinity could feel how snuggly warm she was in her winter down coat.

She knew Garrett was right there behind her as she walked over to the sofa in the cozy living room, and she lifted her gaze to him as he closed the door. He was dressed all cop—tall, sexy. This was worse than she could have imagined. He took in the room and dragged his hands over his face, and she could hear the scrape of whiskers. He had the look of having gone two days without shaving, which only added to all his hotness.

"You know, Dawn never mentioned you having a baby," he said. "Neither did your dad or your mom, and considering they're always talking about you two, about Scott, about all your family…" He let it hang.

She could see his confusion, how he was trying to make sense of this, which was exactly what she didn't want.

He gestured to the baby with his chin. "A newborn…he or she?" he asked as he strode up closer, and she had to pull her gaze away, because she wondered if he could see it in her eyes. She stared at her baby. Could she have picked out that she was his?

"She's a girl," she said, deliberately not commenting on the fact that she was now just over six weeks old. She hoped his math skills weren't as good as she thought they were. Then there was the issue of her parents not knowing about the baby. "Look, my mom and dad don't know, so they would have no reason to say anything to you."

She didn't miss the look of confusion on his face —no, the look of shock. She thought he laughed as he gave his head a shake, just something he did, that expression he had called her out on her bullshit with him one too many times. It was a side of him she had never liked.

"Are you telling me your family has no idea you have a baby? Are you insane, Trinity? Who does something like that?" He gestured to her. "Oh, wait a second. Dawn knows. Of course she does. You wouldn't keep this from Dawn." The way he said it sounded so accusatory, and he was looking at her as if trying to solve a mystery. "Seriously, your sister, the way she was acting, I knew something was way off. She kept showing up today, hanging around the office, wanting me to come up here when she should've been talking to your dad. But my question is why me? Why insist on me coming up here?"

This was hitting way too close to home, and she wanted to kick her sister. "Dawn knows, yes. I'll have you know I was going to surprise my parents this Christmas with a granddaughter, but look, snow-storm, so…" She shrugged, because she couldn't think of what else to say. She tried to put all manner of lightness into her tone, still holding her baby, who was sleeping so soundly and didn't have any idea of the fact that her father was standing right there. Garrett was asking the kind of questions she wanted to stop. Why couldn't he be the kind of guy who could just leave and mind his business?

He was shaking his head, and she knew he thought she was ridiculous, but at the same time, he didn't have a clue this was his daughter yet—nor would he ever, if she had her way. She'd get him out of there, dodge the bullet, and then talk to her mom and dad.

"So is that why you acted all weird and didn't want me closing the back door of the Jeep, because I'd see the baby seat or something?" he said. "What gives here, Trinity? No one hides a baby unless they have something to hide. I know your mom and dad. The sheriff is a good man, and I can't help thinking how he'd react, knowing you kept your baby a secret. In fact, I can actually predict his reaction. It makes no sense, Trinity, you not telling your parents. A baby is not the kind of thing you can hide. Why hide it?"

Oh, he was really overthinking. She pressed her bottom teeth into her top lip. He wasn't letting it drop, asking way too many questions. The best thing would be to get him to walk out and leave and convince him not to say anything.

"Okay, yes," she said. "I have my reasons, though they may not make sense to you. You know what, Garrett? They don't have to, because you have no say in my life. I chose not to say anything for…reasons."

Boy, did that sound pathetic.

He crossed his arms, leaned forward, and barked out that rough laugh that told her he was ready to grind her into the ground. "Bullshit!" he said.

There it was.

"No, it's not, and I don't have to convince you or explain my life to you. Because you have no say in my life. You don't get an opinion, nothing. So you think I'm ridiculous? Fine, I get it, and I heard you, but let me be clear: I am telling my mom and dad, so I'll ask you to please keep my baby's existence to yourself. They don't need you flapping your gums about business that isn't yours. After the storm passes, I'll drive down and introduce them to their granddaughter."

He was staring at her. His toque was the same brown as his deputy uniform and winter coat. What was it about the uniform that cranked up all that hotness? He was one sexy, too-attractive-for-his-own-good male. She'd forgotten how brown his eyes were, too, big and bold, with thick lashes. They were the kind of eyes that carried far too much confidence, the same ones she stared down into every day, her baby's eyes.

She had to pull in another breath, patting her baby's bottom. "So if I can trust you not to say anything, if you could just tell my family I'm snowed in, and…"

The way he was looking at her, she could feel all that alpha male annoyance. He was shaking his head again as if shutting her down with that one motion. What a stubborn asshole he could be. "You seem to be mistaken if you think I'm driving away without you," he said. "You have a baby. For God's sake, Trinity, in case the common sense everyone is born with has completely missed you, you're in the middle of fucking nowhere, and there's a snowstorm. It's freezing, and you're completely cut off, with no cell service to call for help or get out if something happens."

He stopped talking and narrowed his gaze, and her heart thudded, fearing what he would say next. "You know, what I'd like to know is where the father is. Is the reason you said nothing to your family that they hate him or something? Yeah, I can tell by your face I'm getting closer. I mean, where is he?" He took another step into the room and looked around, still carrying that holstered gun. Sweat pooled across her back even though it wasn't warm in the cottage.

For a minute, she had to press her lips together. Then she realized, just maybe, this would be the way to get him to leave. "I'll have you know there is a father, and he lives here too," she said. "He just made a run into town, and I'm sure he'll be back anytime, so you don't have to stay. In fact, he really wouldn't take kindly to you hanging around. He's kind of jealous, and…what are you doing?"

He was looking around, nosy, opening cupboards. Then he walked into her small bathroom, with its tub-shower combo, and then into her bedroom, where he flicked on the light before turning back to her.

"Really, so the baby's father is in town and expected back, yet your Jeep is now stuck in a snowdrift, and when I drove in, there were no tracks going out. I had to clear a path with my truck. Let me also remind you of your story. You're going to your parents' for Christmas, so you were…what, trying to drive out alone? I can't see any man worth anything letting you do that in a snowstorm. You forget what I do for a living, Trinity. I'm a cop. I notice things, and nothing says a man lives here, no shaving cream, razor, or clothes. I know when someone's lying, too, and that's all you've been doing from the moment I drove in here." He opened her closet, and she followed him into her room, trying to think of what to say.

"Okay, fine, he doesn't live here. That's why I didn't say anything to my family. You're right. It's about the guy. He has his life, and I have my mine, and that's the way I like it, but at the same time, he really is coming back, and he's on his way, so you don't need to stick around."

Garrett made a face and closed her closet, taking in the tiny bedroom with the crib at the foot of her double bed, which was a mess, the duvet in a heap. Making the bed was not on the list of necessities, and she was way too tired.

"Well, I have a better idea," he said. "Give me his number, and I'll call him and tell him I'm taking you to your parents' place. As you said, you two aren't involved. He has his own life, so I'm sure he'd appreciate not having to navigate roads no one should be on. What's his name, anyway? Maybe I know him." He leaned in a bit.

She could feel this spinning out of control,

another lie she'd have to keep track of. "Nick," she spat out, feeling her cheeks burn. She had to look down at her baby. "Yes, his name is Nick, and you don't know him. He's new to the area. In fact, he doesn't even live here. He's from Seattle. He was visiting, and things happened, and oops, I got pregnant, but his life is elsewhere."

She took in the smile that pulled at Garrett's lips, which appeared more like a snarl, and she realized he knew she was lying.

"Yeah, well, give me his number," he said. "I'll call him right now."

He pulled out his cell phone, and she stared at it, pressing her lips together hard. He didn't pull his gaze from her as he took another step closer. With his way of looking at her, she swore he could read her better than anyone. She didn't like it.

"Didn't you say the cell towers are down?" She wanted to pat herself on the back, really piling arrogance into her tone. "I'm pretty sure you can't call him." There was something so satisfying about calling out Garrett, and she couldn't keep a smile from pulling at her lips.

"Nick what?" he replied. "What was his last name, again?"

"What does that matter?" she snapped. Why was it that in moments like this, she couldn't think of anything? All that came to mind were Smith, Pitt, and Ryan, names of stars from the movies she watched.

He didn't pull his gaze from her. "Just can't

explain this feeling that you're blowing smoke up my ass, doing everything you can to get me to leave…"

"Watson," she said, cutting him off. "Nick Watson is his name." She dropped her gaze to her baby, because it was damn uncomfortable, trying to keep a straight face under his scrutiny. Her heart was thumping, and she could feel the sweat pooling under her arms. How could she forget that Garrett was the guy no one could pull anything over on? She'd never forget what an asshole he had been in high school in response to what he called her "bitchy behavior." "So you don't need to stay," she continued, "and as I said, you don't know him. We'll be just fine until he gets here."

"You mean I can't call Nick Watson, you said his name was, from Spokane?

She knew he was trying to trip her up, and she blinked. "Right, I just said that." She turned and gestured to the door, but he unzipped his coat and tossed it over the back of the sofa, then pulled the toque off his head and ran his hand through his messy brown hair. "What are you doing?"

He walked over to her and stopped right in front of her, his gaze dropping again to the baby, a look that lingered a little too long, before landing back on her. "So which is it, Trinity, Seattle or Spokane? … And what's the baby's name?"

Why did it feel as if he was interrogating her? She shut her eyes, mentally cursing, and then flicked them open. "Seattle," she said. "Stop confusing me. And I haven't named my baby yet. I haven't figured out the perfect name for her, and it's taking longer than I expected. A name is so important. It's everything. It's her identity. As you see, having a baby and all of this has me a little rattled, and now you're interrogating me… I'm not a criminal, Garrett, yet you're treating me like one. I wonder how my dad would react, knowing you're talking to me the way you are. He wouldn't be happy."

There it was, that arrogant smile again. "I'd say let's call your dad, but the cell towers are down. Again, Trinity, I know your dad, and he'd be asking the same questions I am, only he'd be demanding answers and wouldn't put up with this bullshit you keep trying to dish out. I'm not a fool. I know something's going on and your story doesn't add up. You seriously haven't named your baby?"

He looked around then, and she took in his long-sleeved tan shirt, the badge pinned to his chest, the magnificence of his broad shoulders and long legs. She had to stop looking, because she could remember now too well that one night she shouldn't have enjoyed as much as she did.

"Look, I don't know why you're lying," he said, "but do us both a favor and just stop. You may as well come clean, because I'm not leaving. You say the father's on his way up here, this Nick Watson. Well, then I'm staying until he gets here. See, we can do this the easy way or the hard way. You say he exists? I'll be the judge of that. It's cold in here. I'll start the fire."

She couldn't believe him, and for a second, she couldn't get her tongue to form a reasonable word.

There was just something about Garrett Franke. He could be so unbelievably stubborn, the kind of guy she'd never been able to convince or sweet talk into anything. They'd always been too volatile together, two different personalities that would never sync. Right now, she knew he'd stay there all night. How was it that one lie seemed to roll right into the next?

She pulled in one breath and then another. "Fine, the truth?" she said, taking him in as he squatted down and opened the woodstove, then started crumpling paper in the box beside it with the kindling, which she knew was low. He didn't look her way as he made quick order of building the fire.

"Please," he said, the word dripping with sarcasm.

She was staring at the solid wall of his back and the way his ass filled out his uniform. "The father isn't on his way because he's not in the picture."

He pulled in a breath, and this time he stood up, brushing his hands together, and turned to her. His brown eyes flickered with an intensity that made her feel damn uncomfortable. "Kind of figured that one out, Trinity. I can't help wondering, if you went to all this trouble to create this elaborate lie and hide a baby even from your family, whether you're hiding something. I can smell it. It's just something that comes with being a cop. I can smell bullshit a mile away, and this secret you have with this baby has me asking myself, now, why would Trinity go to such lengths to keep a baby a secret? What the hell is she up to, and what's really going on? It's a puzzle, a mystery." He winked then. "And I'm fucking good at solving them."

The floor softened, and her heart thudded. She had to remind herself to breathe, because this was going from bad to really, really bad.

Before she could come up with even a last Hail Mary that would work on Garrett, the baby chose that moment to let out a wail. *Thank you, baby!* She really needed to figure out a name for her.

CHAPTER

Six

He swore that Trinity could push his buttons in a way no woman ever had. Not only was she the sheriff's daughter, but she was also a mistake that should never have happened one night the year before, with a few too many beers and a dress that was far too low cut.

Now, she'd gone to great lengths to create a lie that was spinning out of control, and worse, she was only digging herself in deeper. He'd lost count of the people he'd arrested who could lie, and every one of them had had something to hide from him.

He could hear her from the bedroom, where she was saying something to the fussy baby, a baby she didn't even have a name for, as she changed her diaper. He took in the cabin, which was maybe five hundred square feet, tops. It was small, cozy, a place he'd never expected a woman alone with a baby to live.

"So as soon as you finish changing the baby, we're

leaving," he said as he leaned in the doorway. When she stiffened, he didn't know why, but he expected one more lie, because that was what Trinity did. She was living and breathing drama and always had been. "And don't even try to say no, because you know I'll pick you up and toss you in the back of the truck. The word 'no' isn't even part of the equation. You have bags packed. I take it they're in your Jeep?"

He knew they had to be, of course, but he still expected some excuse, because nothing was ever simple and easy as far as Trinity went. Cooperating with him was something she had never done and would never do. They'd always been at each other's throats, fighting, disagreeing, arguing.

"Would it do me any good to say no?" She actually stood up and rested her hands on her hips. Her coat was unzipped now, and he took in the baby kicking her legs and fussing a bit. She had to be cold.

"Glad you figured it out," he replied. That had been way too easy. He gestured to the baby, taking in how spitting mad Trinity appeared. "Finish with the baby and get her dressed. Again, everything is in your Jeep?" He made sure his tone conveyed without any doubt that he meant business. It was the same one he used with idiots trying to pull something over on him before he cuffed them.

She just rolled her eyes. "It doesn't take a detective to figure that out, considering I was trying to get out of here and drive myself down. Oh, wait. You're just a lowly deputy, not a detective."

How was it that she could push his buttons and

always say things that had him wanting to wrap his hands around her neck and squeeze the life out of her?

"A simple yes or no will do, Trinity," he snapped. "And wrap that baby up. She's cold." He knew he was being an asshole and stepped out of the bedroom.

"Yes, my bags are in the Jeep," she said, giving attitude right back to him.

He stopped with his back to her and rolled his shoulders, reaching for his coat and then pulling it on, followed by his hat. The door to the woodstove was open, his kindling from earlier still ready to go. He started to the door and pulled it open, then stepped outside into the cold. The wind was blowing, and his truck was already covered with snow, the dark setting in.

He started down the steps right when he heard a crack that cut through the air and shot right through him. He knew that sound all too well, and he looked up just as a tree came crashing down across the driveway, just missing Trinity's Jeep. She shrieked, and he found himself stepping back inside, taking in her wide eyes and the fear she couldn't hide.

"You okay?" he said.

She had pressed the baby against her in that protective way mothers did. It was a side of her he wasn't familiar with. She nodded, and he could see she was having trouble talking, but her expression said everything. "What was that?"

"A tree came down," he replied. "Stay here. I'm going to check it out."

He didn't wait for her to say anything before he stepped back outside and down the steps, through the deep snow, over to her Jeep. The tree was one big-ass motherfucker, lying right across where he needed to drive out. It had missed her Jeep by maybe ten feet.

He pulled his flashlight from his pocket and flicked it on, taking in the trees around them, which he could just make out, as the heavy snow that was covering them was still coming down. One tree was way too close to the cabin for his liking, but as he walked over to the fallen tree, it took him only a second to realize there was no way they were getting out any time soon. He'd need a chainsaw and some help, and even then, it would take a few hours, and the roads were no longer driveable.

Garrett flicked off his flashlight and pulled open the back of her Jeep, seeing two bags and what looked like a portable crib. He lifted them out and shut the back, then started to the cabin. He stamped his feet on the wooden porch and juggled the bags as he opened the door and stepped inside.

What was it about Trinity's eyes? The green was so distinct, so different from Dawn's and her mom's. Everything she was feeling was always right there on the surface. He forced himself to look away as he kicked the door closed and then dumped the bags on the floor. The lights flickered.

"A tree's down right across the road. Looks like we could lose power. You got candles?" he said, but just then, the entire cabin went dark. Great. It seemed as if everything was going from bad to worse. He pulled out his flashlight again and flicked it on.

"Yes, in the kitchen," she said.

He shrugged out of his coat and tossed it on the sofa. "Here, give me the baby, and you get the candles," he said. He wasn't sure what to make of her expression or the way she stiffened, but he held out his arms and gestured. "I don't live here, Trinity. You know where the candles are, and the matches. I assure you I can hold a baby. Go get them, because we need to get some light in here and get a fire started."

She finally relented and slid the baby into his arms. She was tiny, but her eyes were open, and she was staring up at him. He rested his hand protectively on her and wasn't sure what to make of Trinity as he handed her the flashlight.

"We aren't getting out of here tonight, by the looks of things," he said. "We'll need a chainsaw to cut up the tree, and mine is at home. We have only one for the sheriff's department, and I'm pretty sure your dad has it. At the same time, it's cold, and the temperature's dropping. You've got a baby here, so we need to get a fire going."

She was already in the kitchen, rummaging through a drawer. He listened to the flick of a match and watched as she lit candles, then a kerosene lamp on a cabinet behind the sofa. At least there was light.

"I have a chainsaw in the woodshed out back, but I'm out of oil for the fuel mix," she said. "This is just fantastic. So you're saying my peaceful, quiet Christmas alone isn't going to happen." She set the glass top back on the lamp and flicked off his flash-light. She was still wearing her bomber jacket, and he could really feel the chill as he slid the baby back into her arms. Touching her was unavoidable, but she wouldn't look up at him.

"The fire's ready to go," he said. "Saw you have some wood on the porch. Hope you have more."

She gestured outside with her chin. "The woodbox on the porch has just a few pieces, but the woodshed is behind the house, and there's likely half a cord left. The ax and everything is out there. I have a battery-operated lantern in the cupboard by the fridge." She was looking everywhere except at him, and he just couldn't figure out what the deal was with her. Then she finally met his eyes. "So what you're saying is that I'm stuck here with you, and there's no way out. There's no way for you to leave…"

He wondered if she'd always been like this. Yeah, there was tension, but she seemed more nervous than usual. "We've been through this," he said. "I'm not leaving you up here alone. So, if you need plain English, I'll give it to you: There's a huge tree across the road, a few feet of snow, and more still falling. The chainsaw in your shed is without fuel, and the cell towers are down. We're trapped. There's no way down. So I'll get the fire started, go cut some wood, see if the radio is working in the truck, and radio into the office. At least then your dad will know you're safe, and I guess then you can answer a few more of my questions."

He shrugged on his coat and pulled on his hat, then pulled open the door.

Trinity had gone quiet. Yeah, there always had been one thing about her: Her face told him everything she was thinking and feeling—and now, it said she was hiding a lot.

The heat from the woodstove was starting to warm the cabin. Garrett had started the fire, but where was he now but out in his truck? From what Trinity could see, it seemed he was talking to someone, and that someone was likely her dad. He was likely telling him all about her big secret, the baby her parents didn't know about.

What was it about secrets? She'd wanted to control this on her terms, but it was now blowing up in her face in ways she'd never expected. Maybe that was why she was standing at the window, the baby cooing in her arms, as she stared out that single pane at Garrett. For the life of her, she didn't have a clue what he was saying. Damn him, already, and damn her sister for sending him out there!

She glanced down at the baby and heard the truck door close, and she lifted her gaze to see him coming back to the cabin. He came up the porch with heavy footsteps and stomped his feet before opening the door, bringing snow and cold. She could hear the whistle of the wind. Apparently, things were starting to pick up.

His gaze lingered a moment on her. "You'll be happy to know the radio works. I spoke with Rose, who patched your dad in, so he knows that you're not coming, I'm here with you, and you're fine. He's going to send up help in the morning when the storm dies down."

She wasn't sure what expression was on her face as she swayed with the baby. Garrett slid off his coat and rested it over one of the two straight-back wooden chairs at the small table, then pulled off his toque and tossed it down as well. His back was to her.

Did he have any idea how good he looked? He wasn't average by any means, but then, he never had been. He'd always set himself apart from everyone—rugged, drop-dead fucking gorgeous. Everything about the way he carried himself had women giving him a second and third look. Of course he knew. Guys like that always did.

Arrogant asshole.

It took her a second to realize he had turned around and was watching her in that all-cop way of his, and she had to fight the urge to turn away. It was a look she was familiar with, having grown up with a father who was the sheriff of Idaho Falls. That was something they did, always trying to figure people out, to see what people were hiding as if they already knew the truth. She didn't like feeling as if she was entirely at his mercy.

"Don't worry," he said. "I didn't say anything about the baby."

She let out a breath that, even to her own ears, sounded like relief. She didn't miss the hint of amusement on his face. "Well, I guess I can thank you for that."

"Oh, not sure I'd want to be in your shoes, though, telling your dad now. It's quite the bomb to drop. I know Julia and Logan well enough to suspect that this is the kind of thing where, once they get over the shock, they'll be asking a lot of questions. I still don't understand why you did it. Nothing you've said convinces me in any way that you needed to keep the baby a secret. Like, what were you thinking, never telling your parents? And you really haven't named the baby? Who does that? How old is she?"

He stepped closer, looking at the baby in a way that made her so damn uncomfortable, and then he flicked those questioning eyes back to her. What was it about the color of them, such a deep amber that it reminded her of single-malt whiskey? He was so frickin' alpha that he had her wanting to move back and get out from under his scrutiny. He was definitely the kind of guy who didn't walk away from things.

Her head was spinning as she tried to figure out what to say to him so he wouldn't know the truth. How long would it take him to figure it out? How many questions could she answer? She was sweating, and it wasn't even hot.

He laughed before she could answer. "Damn, girl, you're still working it. You know I can always tell when someone is hiding something. I just asked how old the baby is, and your entire expression shifted. You're freaking out, and I can see the wheels spinning in your brain."

"Six weeks," she said. "Fine, there you go. I just don't understand why you had to come up here. I know how you feel about me, and it's mutual, Garrett. You think I'm a stuck-up bitch, and I know you're an arrogant asshole. I just don't like people in my business."

"You're freaking out again. There you go," he stated, then held his arms out for the baby, whom she instinctively held tighter. "Relax. Seriously, Trinity. I'm not sure what's up with you, but I'll hold the baby so you can take off your coat."

She wasn't sure how he did it, but the baby was now in the cradle of his arms. She was so tiny, how she fit into the crook of one elbow. She didn't like the way he was watching her, the way he was holding her, so confident. She wondered if men ever knew when something was theirs.

"You know what I don't get, Trinity, is you staying up here alone," Garrett said. "You say there's no father in the picture, but why not tell Logan and Julia? It's not as if they're the kind of people who'd lose it and wouldn't understand. They'd have helped you out, been up here with you. It just doesn't make sense. Why? Could it be about the father, the circumstances, or what? There has to be something you haven't said to explain this, because to me, this is all nonsense."

Maybe that was why her heart was thumping and her hands were sweating. He was apparently going to be true to his word and interrogate the hell out of her.

"Well, as you've already pointed out to me numerous times, Garrett, you evidently don't understand the fact that I like my privacy. You don't get me. I just never expected to find myself pregnant…"

The expression on his face was priceless and had her wanting to bite her tongue. "Privacy from your parents? Bullshit, Trinity. You seem to forget I work for your dad, and I know Dawn and your family. You just keep tossing out excuses like you think if you spit out enough versions of a story, I'll finally buy it. See, the thing is, Trinity, once you start lying, I'm expecting everything you say to be bullshit. So let's break it down. I can do this all night, you know."

She rolled her shoulders and could feel the stress, wishing the baby would cry or something so she could take her back, feed her, and not have to look at all that handsomeness staring back at her.

"The father, is he someone your parents know?"

Her heart thudded, and she ran her hand over her hat and pulled it off, feeling the static in her long dark hair, which she knew had to be a mess. She swept it back with her hand.

"Okay, not answering," Garrett said. "I take it he is. Does he live in Idaho Falls? Is his name even Nick? Too many questions all at once?" It was in his eyes, the way he was studying her.

She had to find a way to get him off this line of questioning. "Look, I may have fudged some details, but rest assured, my parents will understand once I tell them."

He laughed. He still had the baby but took a step away, walking around her. "I doubt that very much, Trinity." He was really looking at the baby, and he said nothing for a second. Something about the way he looked at her had Trinity wanting to grab the baby from his arms. When he lifted his gaze, his expression had her stomach dropping to her knees. "It was last year you and I hooked up," he said. "I remember it clearly. Right after the new year, wasn't it? Or…right, it was that party your sister threw, in the spring. Your parents were out of town."

He gave everything to the baby, and she wanted to shut her eyes and step back out of this moment, as she knew he knew, and she didn't have a clue how to lie her way out of it.

"Is she mine?" he finally said. He didn't look at Trinity. Maybe he could see some of the resemblance.

"Don't be ridiculous," she said. "Of course she's not, and that was…"

When his gaze landed on her, it was far from friendly. It was filled with so much anger, as if he was sick of her messing with him. "Don't you dare start bullshitting me on this, Trinity, because that's all you've been doing since I showed up here. Now it's starting to add up, the way you've been acting, trying to hide the baby, the secrets, the lies. What the fuck…?"

She reached out to take the baby, as she had started fussing, and for just a second, she thought he'd refuse. "Garrett, seriously, give me my baby."

He finally relented, but he slid his hand over her arm, then under her chin, making her look at him as she held her baby. "This can go one of two ways, Trinity. I can tell by your face that I've just figured it all out. There are DNA tests, a simple blood test. I can make you do it. Is that how you want this to go? I can take this all the way, and I will get my answer one way or the other."

Oh, fuck! This was exactly what she didn't want to happen.

She shut her eyes and pulled in a breath. "Fine, truth time," she said. "She's yours, but at the same time, Garrett, what do you think my dad is going to do to you when he finds out that his deputy was messing around with his daughter?"

She wasn't sure what expression was on his face, but one thing was sure: She'd just opened up a can of worms, and it wasn't lost on her that this was the first time since Garrett had shown up that he was absolutely speechless.

"Well, I can tell by your face that you now understand why I did what I did," she said. "You see, it's best for everyone if this baby remains not yours, so I'm doing you a favor." She wanted to pat herself on the back as she took in the way he stood there, hand on hip.

He pulled his other hand over his jaw, then gestured to her. "Yet again I'm hearing bullshit," he said, leaning in, "and if you think you're keeping my daughter from me, you've got another thing coming."

CHAPTER
Eight

What was it about hearing something he'd never expected to hear in a million years? Garrett felt as if a bomb had been dropped in his lap. Being a cop, he figured he'd seen and heard everything, from the odd, to the unusual, to the really stupid that had him merely shaking his head. But this was beyond anything he could ever have imagined.

His daughter.

His baby.

He could just make out Trinity in the candlelight as she walked over to the woodstove, carrying the baby in one arm and a pot of water in the other. She rested it on the stove and then walked back into the kitchen, where she opened the fridge and pulled out a bottle as the baby fussed.

"What are you doing?" It was all he could think to ask. She hesitated, maybe from his tone, but right now he was having to fight the urge to wrap his hands around her neck and squeeze.

She lifted the bottle and continued walking, her expression filled with sass. "Thought it was obvious. I'm heating a bottle. The baby's hungry." She cooed to the baby, and he was stuck on so many things running through his mind. The baby was his, from a one-nighter, and she'd never said one word to him.

"You don't nurse?" he said.

She had her back to him, but then she turned, and her eyes were filled with that "drop dead" look she'd mastered. "So because I'm a woman, I'm supposed to nurse my baby?"

He laughed. She had to know she was pushing his buttons. "Not what I said, Trinity, so don't put words in my mouth. It was a simple question, although I can't understand why you wouldn't. Seems it would be easier."

She made a rude noise. "I guess, being a man, you'd think so, but it's not as easy as you'd think, and it didn't work for me, having sore boobs, with the baby not getting enough and everyone criticizing me…"

"Who was criticizing you? You live up here alone. Who have you even told about the baby? Remember, you've kept her a secret." He just couldn't help calling her out. She'd always been way overdramatic with everything. He knew he was getting loud, and he took in the face she made.

"It was a general comment," she snapped. "Okay, so a nurse said it. You want me to get specific?

Anyway, I did my own research, and I'll have you know that nursing a baby isn't the be-all and end-all. Maybe I'm just oversensitive on the matter, but besides, it's my choice, and neither you nor anyone else has a say."

He wanted to laugh at her again, but instead he leveled her with the gaze he used on criminals who dished out stupid excuses, thinking he'd buy them. Then he lifted his hands. "You know what? That works for me. It'll make it easier for me. I'll be able to feed my daughter myself and not have to rely on you."

He wasn't sure what to make of her face, her expression. Alarm or something. "Excuse me?" she said, then shook her head, at a loss for words. Then she seemed to pull it together. "I'm sorry, but what are you talking about? She's my daughter. I'm not sure where you seem to think you'll be feeding her. The storm will be over, and you even said tomorrow that my dad is coming up. I'll deal with my parents, but they'll never know you're the father."

He leaned in again, allowing his gaze to drop to his daughter, who had her tiny fist crammed in her mouth and was sucking and fussing, before lifting his gaze and taking Trinity in. "You can stop that right now. She's my daughter too, mine, and now that I know, you seriously cannot be under the delusion that I would walk out the door and leave her alone with you."

Her eyes widened, and her breath caught.

He shook his head. "I'll deal with your father and

my actions, but there's no way you're keeping my daughter from me. She'll be in my life, and I won't be just a visitor in hers. There's no way in hell you're living up here alone with my daughter in the middle of nowhere, either, Trinity. You made some reckless choices, and not telling me I had a baby is right up there. It's unforgiveable. You've always been selfish, but denying me my daughter, and her me? I didn't get to be there when she was born, and I missed your entire pregnancy, and now how many weeks of her life? No more. Not one more day will pass without me being there for her."

Even in the candlelight, he thought she'd paled. The water was bubbling now on the woodstove, so he lifted it, seeing the steam, and pulled out the bottle, which was now likely too warm. He dumped the pot in the sink and walked back into the room, seeing how tightly she held the baby.

"You can't honestly think I would let you have any part in her life, Garrett," she said. "I'm her mother."

He leaned in again, and she went to reach for the bottle, but he pulled his hand back. "And I'm her father," he said. "If I were you, I wouldn't push me on this, Trinity, because I won't go quietly into the night. I know very well how the law works, and I will, if push comes to shove and you try to keep her from me, hire a lawyer and get custody of her. I won't be pushed out of her life, and I will not let you keep her from me, not one more day. You've already done that, Trinity."

A tear slipped down her cheek. "Are you trying to take my daughter from me?" she said.

Just hearing the emotion in her voice had him feeling like an asshole, and this time, when she reached for the bottle, he let her have it. "No, Trinity, but at the same time, I will not allow you to keep doing what you've been doing, keeping her from me."

It was the first time since being here that he could see something in her that resembled fear. She seemed so uncertain now, or maybe he'd never really understood how she ticked at all.

Trinity flicked some of the milk from the bottle onto her arm and then settled the bottle into the baby's mouth. She was sucking and making all kinds of squeaky noises, and he took another second to see all of his daughter. She was his. She was so small, and it terrified him for a second, her being up here alone in the middle of nowhere, in a storm. Anything could have happened.

"I'm not sure I'm liking how this is sounding, Garrett. I live up here, my daughter lives here, and we love it up here."

He didn't nod, but he did pull in a breath. "Well, then there's a problem, because I leave tomorrow, and the baby is coming. So I guess you have a choice to make: You can decide to stay up here alone, or…" He stopped talking and took in Trinity and the baby. He could see the moment what he was saying sank in.

"Or what, Garrett? This is starting to sound like a threat, like you want to take my baby from me. How could you be so cruel?"

"I'm not trying to be cruel, Trinity, but you're not walking all over me. You know you can't do that with me. I have a nice house in town, and I want my baby in my house, living under my roof, where I can take care of her."

Her face was a mosaic of emotions. She was so damn stubborn. "And what about me? I'm…what, to be a passing visitor?"

He knew she didn't get it. He could see her confusion. "No, Trinity, that's not what I'm saying. She's my baby, and you're her mother, so whether you or I like it, we're in each other's lives forever. Where she goes, you'll go."

"I'm not sure I understand what you're saying. You want me to live under your roof with you?"

He exhaled. "No. What I want is for you and me to get married—and she needs a name."

He wasn't sure who was more surprised, her or him. Instead of saying something, she started laughing.

S he stood in the doorway of the only bedroom in her cabin. The baby was now fast asleep in her crib, and she'd lingered as long as she could, covering her with a quilt and staring at her, her little bundle of joy, not sure how to handle the big alpha in the next room, who was literally laying down the law.

There was just something about Garrett. He had never allowed her to manipulate, play, or walk over him in any way. And it was absolutely frustrating. Guys had always wanted to do anything for her, except Garrett, who had always given her the impression he hated everything about her. Standing in the shadow of his confidence made her feel uneasy.

"Are you going to stand in the doorway all night?" he said, as he shoved another piece of wood in the woodstove. "We have things to settle. Get on out here, Trinity."

She could hear the crackle of wood and made

herself step into the open room as he stood up. He'd taken off his belt with his holstered gun, cuffs, and all the cop gear he carried, and his sleeves were rolled up. She took in the tattoo of a dagger with a snake wrapped around it on his forearm. It was the kind of tattoo that spoke volumes about who he was, a man who never shied away from any fight.

He tracked her every step with his eyes, radiating strength. He was immovable, not to be pushed around by anyone. What the hell was she going to do? Her heart was hammering with each step she took, not so much from fear as from the fact that everything she'd kept closely guarded seemed to be unraveling and she couldn't stop any of it.

"Fine, we have things to settle," she said. "You want to talk about names for the baby?"

She was literally freaking out, though, because he'd suggested—no, stated that he wanted them to get married. The man was seriously out of his mind, and it wasn't something she wanted to have on the table, not with Garrett.

"I said other things too, but yeah, let's start with a name. My mother's name was Mary Esther, Mary for short. I think that would be a great name." He crossed his arms, and the muscles flexed in his forearms. He seemed to think that was the end of discussion.

"You want to name my baby—"

"Our baby. Get that straight, Trinity. She's ours, yours and mine, or are you going to claim again that she's not? You want to play it that way, I told you already, all it takes is a simple DNA test."

The way he said it, she knew he was digging in, and she had no doubt he would drag her kicking and screaming from her comfort zone with the baby she'd been too chicken to tell anyone about. He wasn't about to let her wade in carefully. She knew that about him, because Garrett Franke didn't wade in anywhere; he jumped off the deep end.

"Fine, point made. Yes, she's yours, and I know that because unlike you, I wasn't hopping into bed with the next available warm body," she said, and she wasn't sure what to make of his face. She hadn't wanted to go down that road, telling him she knew about all the women he'd slept with after her. "But we're talking about the baby and her name, so let's put the rest of that on the back burner. I'm not naming her after your mother. She's an individual. It's her name, and it's important, permanent. It says who she is. We're not naming her Mary Esther."

He was watching her, and she had to fight the urge to fidget. "Then give me your list of names, because this is ridiculous. She needs a name. Also, you're making me sound like some man whore, which I'm not. I'm single. I did not have a long list of women in my bed." He stated it so directly, so calmly, and she knew well that he'd keep at it until he got what he wanted. He didn't seem to forget about anything, but Trinity knew all about Lori, who, according to Dawn, had her hooks in Garrett.

"I don't have a list," she said. "I try out names, Olivia, Skye, Mia…but nothing is her. It'll come to me. I just need to give it some time." She had to fight the urge to fidget again. What was it about the way he stared at her? She swore he knew what she was thinking. She had to cross her arms and then let them fall to her sides, fisting her hands under his scrutiny. *Damn nerves.*

"In how many more weeks? It still hasn't come to you, and she needs a name. You can't keep calling her 'Baby.' You're not being fair to her. You don't want to call her Mary? Fine. I'll give you a choice of three names, and you pick one. If you don't, I will."

Was he serious?

"Skye, Mia, or Chloe," he rattled off, holding up a finger for each. Even when he spoke, it felt so much like a demand, as if he were gearing up for a fight. She could feel the ultimatum, and she knew her jaw slackened. She was likely staring at him like a fool.

"You can't expect me to choose a name just like that, as if you're putting a gun to my head. You're not being fair, Garrett."

He raised his eyebrows, and his expression was so hard, so unsympathetic. The face he made was decisive. Good Lord, the man could stand his ground like no one she'd ever met. "Fine," he said. "Mia it is."

She could feel him ripping away her choice. "No, no, no," she said. "She is not a Mia. Skye is her name."

A smile touched the edges of his lips as if he'd managed to maneuver her right where he wanted.

"You wanted Skye all along!" she said. She knew she sounded accusatory, and he didn't even have the grace to appear sheepish. Nope, confident and arrogant was exactly who Garrett was.

He shrugged. "The thing with you, Trinity, is that giving you too many choices is the same as giving you enough rope to hang yourself."

"That's cruel, Garrett," she said, unsure what to make of the way he was watching her.

"No, cruel is what you're doing, living up here, hiding out, keeping Skye from her father, me, and your family. I just can't figure out why you do what you do, why you go to such lengths, digging yourself into a situation that quickly goes from bad to worse. But I do know if you're left to your own devices, it's a recipe for disaster. So, our daughter has a name, Skye Esther Franke."

She couldn't believe he'd snuck that in there, and she started to protest when he held up his hand.

"Uh-uh," he said. "I can see where this is going. You'll start arguing, and then we'll be right back to the baby having no name. You named her, her first name, so her middle name is after my mother."

"I'm not giving her your last name," she said. "That's so old fashioned. She already has my last name, Cooper Wilde. It's a good name and works just fine."

He raised a brow. "I'm her father. She's having my name. Hate to tell you this, but it's not negotiable, Trinity. You want to argue about it, okay, let's do it, bring it on, but you won't win. My daughter, my name. Maybe to you it's old fashioned, but in case you've forgotten, she's mine, and you kept her from me, and I'm not willing to bend on that. You've denied me how much time of her existence—over a month? Then there was the entire time you were pregnant. And just so we're clear, we're getting married, too. Yeah, you thought I'd forget, let you manipulate the conversation and steer it how you want it. You seem to forget I know all your tricks."

Her stomach dropped to her knees again. Holy shit, he really had her cornered. She didn't like the feeling and lifted her hands. "You can't expect me to marry you just because there's a baby. That's absolutely ridiculous, Garrett. That's not a good enough reason to get married."

It was in his entire presence, as if he was convinced this was the only way. "It's a start, Trinity, and of course I expect us to get married because there's a baby. It's more than enough of a reason. There're others, too."

She was positive her face lost color as she stared at this stubborn, pig-headed, drop-dead gorgeous man. "Really, then how about this for a reason? We're not getting married because the minute you finished with me, how many days later did I see you making eyes at Lori Drakerman? In fact, even my sister said you've been seeing each other, involved this entire time. I mean, you're practically married already. So no, Garrett, you may be the type to love them and leave them, but I sure as hell am not marrying a man who can replace one woman with another before the bed is even cold."

There it was, surprise, shock. No, he appeared to

snarl as he leaned in again. "Well, guess what? Lori and I aren't together, and you and I both know that night was a mistake between you and me. Then you were gone. And just so we're clear…" He stepped in closer, so close she could feel his heat, taking in all that arrogance. "The town gossip is atrocious. Lori and I were never serious. We were friends. We were certainly never getting married, and there's no commitment between us. We're not even seeing each other anymore."

"So, what, she was some fuck buddy?" she snapped, feeling uncomfortable at the idea of him with someone else. This was really fucking with her head. She wasn't the jealous type, yet here she was, feeling that ugly green-eyed monster poking at her sound reasoning.

He just shook his head. "Look, I'm single. We dated. Call it what you want, but that's all it was. I'm not discussing Lori with you, because there's nothing to discuss. It's over and done. What I am discussing and settling with you is the fact that we have a baby together, which you kept from me. Skye is sleeping in there, and she's mine, so if you're trying to come up with some reason why we can't be married, you're going to have to come up with something better than Lori. A baby equals a commitment, Trinity."

He stepped so close that she was pressed against him, and he slid his hand over her back as he pulled her to him. She thought a squeak slipped past her lips as her hands slapped over his chest. Holy shit! How could she have forgotten the strength that oozed from those pecs, the solid broadness of his chest, which she swore could protect her from anything? He was so close, holding her so close, and he said nothing else for a second.

"Garrett, this is…" She couldn't come up with anything reasonable as she pressed into him. The attraction, the chemistry, had always been there, and she wanted to turn her head, but she couldn't make herself push him away.

"Oh yeah, it's still there," he said. He was such a cocky son of a bitch. The way he was looking down at her, holding her, she felt safe and terrified at the same time, because he made her feel things no one ever had. "You know what? That baby in there, Skye, our daughter, deserves a father and a mother, and this here…"

He lowered his head, and she knew what was coming and was so angry for wanting it so much. He pressed a kiss to her lips, but it wasn't just a kiss. It was deep and scorching, the kind of kiss she'd experienced only from Garrett, the man she had sworn she was born to kiss. Instead of pushing him away, her hands fisted in his shirt, holding him there as she found herself drowning in that kiss. She leaned into him, and her knees weakened. She'd have slid right to the floor if he hadn't been holding her. Then he broke the kiss and lifted his head just a bit, his breath warm on her face.

"There's chemistry, heat, whatever you want to call it," he said. "That's more than enough to base a marriage on, with a baby already here."

She didn't know how she did it, but she managed to push him away and step back even though her body wanted nothing more than to be in his arms again. "No, no, no," she said. "You're not hearing me, Garrett. I'm not marrying you. I don't care what you say. You can't make me. There's nothing you do or say that would have me signing away my freedom and getting hitched to the likes of you…"

Then he was smiling and gave that familiar rough, arrogant laugh that had her fisting her hands.

"What?" she snapped. "Why are you laughing?"

"Oh, Trinity, you're wrong there. I do know something, and that something is called your dad. How do you think he'll react, knowing you kept your baby from him and your mom, hid up here alone, and didn't tell the father—you know, me—that I had a daughter? He'll be angry."

She lifted her hands and felt flustered, but something about the way he was looking at her had her thinking he had something else up his sleeves. "I know he'll be angry, and my mom too, but they'd never make me marry you. No one can make me do anything I don't want to do. It's my choice. You know, free will?"

"Right, but they will make you do the right thing. They'll keep at you and sit you down and have that hard talk with you, especially after I go to your dad and put it all out on the table about how I asked you to marry me, how I plan to take care of you and the baby. Just so you understand, Trinity, I'm not going anywhere, and your dad will be the first one to tell you that I mean what I say. He knows I'm like a dog with a bone. When I said we're getting married, I mean it. I will keep at you until you give in. My baby is going to live under my roof, with a mother and a father.

"Don't fight me on this one, Trinity, because if I go for custody of our daughter, any judge will make sure I get it. In case you need a reminder, you kept her from me, and that kind of deceit isn't looked on kindly. You want to play hardball? I can do that, but what I won't do is let this continue. You've always had guys wrapped around your finger, doing what you wanted. You think I couldn't see? But that's not the way to handle you, Trinity. I think you know already I'm not the kind of guy you can manipulate or become evasive with. So what is it going to be, Trinity, the easy way or the hard way?"

She just stared at Garrett, wondering how it was possible to love a man and hate him at the same time. "You're pushing me, Garrett, trying to corner me, but I'm not going to be pushed around and told how to think or what to do. If you want to fight, bring it on, because I'm not marrying you. Nothing you say will have me letting you put a ring on my finger."

Instead of saying anything else, Trinity walked into the bedroom and closed the door.

Garrett had to fight the urge to put his fist in something hard, a wall, anything. Instead, he swore under his breath, having to dig really deep to pull it together. Trinity could trigger every one of his alpha male instincts.

She'd never been easy. He'd heard that over and over from Logan, his boss, who he knew had struggled with Trinity more so than Dawn. At the same time, he was well aware of the event that had scarred Trinity so deeply and had her treading so carefully into everything: She'd been kidnapped as a kid by her teacher, and it had completely rocked the community.

Logan had saved her, but she'd never been the same. Garrett had seen it all through school, how everyone had treated her with kid gloves and made excuses for every outburst or meltdown, how she had been allowed to get away with things anyone else would be scolded for. He could give her a minute now, and he knew that was all anyone ever did.

He forced himself to take another second to pull it together. He locked up the front door, looking out the tiny single-pane window and taking in the darkness. He could just make out the heavy snow still coming down.

In the tiny kitchen were an old electric stove, a fridge, and a few old cabinets. Everything about this cabin was small, quaint. He took another second to see it as the hideout that it was as he blew out the candles and stuck the matches on the counter into his pocket. He shoved more wood in the woodstove and closed up the damper, then blew out the rest of the candles in the living room, leaving just the kerosene lamp burning. Then he blew out that too and flicked on the battery-operated lantern.

For a second, he just listened to the silence, hearing the whistle of the wind and the winter storm that had settled in around them. Then he stepped to the closed bedroom door and rested his hand on the knob.

When he opened the door, Trinity had kicked off her boots and was sitting on the edge of the small double bed, near the crib with Skye, his daughter. Her wavy dark hair was long and loose, and she was wearing a sweater and blue jeans. Not a word was said. It was just her and him, and he set the lantern on the small bedside table.

"What are you doing?" She frowned, forming a crease in her brow.

"Not giving you a minute," he said. "You seem to have a way about you, Trinity. You push people away, and they let you, thinking you just need space. But look what happens when you get it." He could see the moment her back went up. "Don't start reading what I'm saying the wrong way."

He stepped over to the crib and leaned down, seeing his daughter in her sleeper, sucking on a soother, fast asleep, a knit hat covering her soft brown hair. She'd kicked off the blanket, and he lifted it and covered her again, feeling the chill in the air.

"She's so small," he said. He leaned on the rail, taking her in, hearing the creak of the bed behind him before Trinity stepped over, closer, and stopped right beside him. She ran her hand on the rail. It was so close to his arm that he could have reached over and touched her.

"She was six pounds, four ounces when she was born," she said.

He just took her in and had to fight the urge to ask something as he took in what she wasn't saying. She was so uneasy, something else she was struggling with. "Was it an easy birth? You were alone up here and pregnant. Where was she born?"

She pulled in a breath. The room was dim, and the light from the lantern behind them gave off a soft glow, but he could see something in her that he wondered if anyone else saw. Fear. She was scared. It seemed as if it was a part of her, controlling her.

"I stayed up here," she said. "Dawn was here and planned to stay with me for the last few weeks before I was due. She'd just arrived, and it was on the first night when I went into labor early. She drove us down in the first snowfall. Skye was born in Meridian, after nine hours of labor, if you call that easy…" She shrugged.

He didn't know what to say. "I wasn't there, Trinity. That's why I'm asking. Meridian…" He shook his head, seeing that she really had gone out of her way to keep the baby from him. "I don't understand why you didn't tell me. You should have told me as soon as you found out you were pregnant."

"So you could have done right by me?" She turned and stepped away, and he thought she was going to walk out of the bedroom as he leaned on the rail of the crib. There was something about this tiny little innocent baby. He'd never felt so damn helpless in his life, and he wanted nothing more than to protect her from everything.

"You're damn right I would have," he said.

Trinity stopped in the doorway, her back to him, and she rested her hand on the frame. He was positive, just for a second, he could see her hand shaking. What the hell was she so scared of?

"I'm right here, Trinity, and I'm not going anywhere," he said. "You can keep pushing and pushing, but I'm not going anywhere. You should know it doesn't work that way with me."

Then she turned around, and even in the shadow of the cabin, he could see she was struggling to hide her emotions. "No, but you want to take my baby from me."

He glanced once to the baby and then turned and faced her, taking one step to close the distance, carefully, and then another. "No, I do not want to take her from you. I said we're getting married, but you've thrown up every obstacle, trying to push me away, even going so far as to hide her from me, from your family. For what? Because you're terrified, I can see it, but I don't understand what you're scared of."

It was as if, just by bringing it up, he had summoned it into the room with them. How the hell did she live up here alone? She wasn't just scared; she was petrified. She said nothing, and he could see how uneasy she was.

"You can't even tell me, can you?" he said. "So how did you do it up here, alone, being so scared? This isn't normal, Trinity, hiding out, not facing life. You're not a little girl anymore, and it's almost as if you think this is going to keep you safe. I wonder if you even know what it is you're scared of."

She opened her mouth, but nothing came out at first. "You don't get it, Garrett…"

"Then explain it to me, because I've watched from the sidelines for years, seeing you for who you really are."

"A spoiled brat, a troublemaker, a fuckup?" Her voice caught.

He frowned and took another step, then another, until he stood right in front of her. He lifted his hand and brushed back her hair to tuck it behind her ear. She shut her eyes, and he could feel her trembling.

"No, I never saw you as that," he said. When she

flicked open her eyes, they were filled with such raw emotion. "Everyone was scared to push you, worried that you would break, and I watched, seeing how you took it and just did whatever Dawn wanted you to do even when it wasn't what you wanted. Everyone was too easy on you, Trinity, after you were kidnapped. I remember, still living next door to your parents' house, it scared the hell out of everyone in the community. That's one of the reasons I'm a cop today. That one moment shaped you and everything you're doing now."

She frowned. "You became a cop because of me?"

"Yeah, because someone could just walk into a tight-knit community like ours, a stranger, and fit in so well, and no one questioned anything about him. But after you were back, you weren't the same, and every outburst, every meltdown, had people babying you and giving you whatever you wanted…"

"Except you," she said.

He rested his hands on her shoulders and just held them there, feeling her breath. "That wasn't what you needed."

"What do you know about it? You were so cruel. I could feel how you hated me…"

He shook his head. "Is that how you see it? I called you out on all your crap. I wouldn't let you get away with anything. That's not hate. I never hated you, but I wasn't about to be another person who just looked past everything you did, every unreasonable outburst, every mistake, every time you would snap at someone, say something thoughtless, demand something, become selfish, or act out. Every time, I saw you had figured out how to use what happened to you to get what you figured you needed. You had figured out how to get everyone to toe the line with you.

"Remember that class project in high school, you got first pick, but then you changed your mind and got to choose a topic someone else had already picked? I didn't hate you, but I disliked what you did. It wasn't right. At the same time, what was worse was how the teachers and townsfolk all made exceptions just for you. The only one who never did was me. I wasn't jumping in that crap, because that's not the way to handle you."

He slid his hand over her cheek, under her chin, and then let it fall away, and she didn't move. She pulled her gaze away, though, and looked to the side, frowning, considering.

"And you think the way to handle me is to bully me?" she said. "To give me no choice?"

He just took a second to really see her and how unsettled she was. "It's called a firm hand, Trinity," he replied. "You don't respond to someone letting you have choices, because you avoid them and don't face anything. I don't know how you did it up here alone, but bullying is not how I see it. I will not—and let me be very clear—allow you to stay up here alone with Skye. She's coming home with me. Can I make you marry me? Can I make you live under my roof…?"

He shook his head. "You're right, I can't, but what I can do is make sure my daughter is safe. I swear to God and everything almighty that nothing will happen to her, and I can do that only with her under my roof. Am I being an asshole about it? Of course I am, but you can't handle someone making things easy for you and letting you figure out what's right, because you don't face things. You avoid them. I want you to marry me, but I won't ask and wait for you to decide, because look at you now. You're absolutely terrified and will come up with any excuse for why it can't or won't work. Would you honestly walk away from the baby?"

"No," she snapped, and for a second she seemed to pull into herself. "No, I would never leave her. She's mine."

"She's ours," he said again. "And I'm not asking you to leave her, but she's my daughter too, Trinity."

"I don't want to get married," she said. Behind her words, he could feel a long list of excuses and buts, and he knew anyone else would have just walked away, because that would have been easier.

"You don't know what you want. I'll make you happy." He rested his hand again on her shoulder, rubbing her arm.

"You're too bossy."

"I am, and I'm not going to change," he said.

She shut her eyes, still working her way through the list. "We'd never work. We're like oil and water."

"Don't agree. I won't let you walk all over me. You're terrified, but I won't let anything happen to you. I'll keep you safe, both of you."

She rested both her hands on his chest and squeezed the fabric of his shirt. She was breathing heavy, fast. He could feel her anxiety. "Women want you, lots of women. You'll find someone less complicated, and then you'll leave."

Ah, so there it was. He was getting somewhere.

"I don't want anyone else," he said. "You already know a pretty face can't sway me. I seem to have a thing for complicated pains in the ass. You're not easy, but I will hold on to you with both hands. I won't let anything happen to you." He rubbed her arms, squeezed her shoulders, holding her right there. Her eyes were wide, and he wondered if anyone could see how much she struggled, could see what he saw. "We could keep going, Trinity, but you've got to trust someone. I think you know I'm not going anywhere. You are your own worst nightmare. I wish you could see yourself the way I see you."

He thought there was a hint of a smile.

"As a pain in the ass?" she stated and lifted her gaze as if she was proud of that label.

He inhaled. "There is the outer Trinity that you show the world, and it took a while for me to realize that you started being that way because you think everyone expects it of you and that's the only way to get something. But I see past all that, to the scared, terrified girl who was robbed of a carefree childhood when someone you trusted betrayed you and hurt you. That will never happen to our daughter. I can see deep inside that you just want to be understood for who you really are, but at the same time, you're too terrified to show everyone the real you. You're smart, you have a lot of love to give, and you're a good mother, but you've always been so scared to make a decision, and what everyone can't figure out is that it's because you're afraid of the consequences."

She was going to deny it.

He made himself hold her in his gaze, made her look at him. "I see you, all of you," he said. "Stop being so damn scared around me. No one is going to hurt you. I will not hurt you."

She said nothing. He was reaching her, but she was so much damn work, a challenge the likes of which he'd never encountered. He wondered whether she had any idea how deep her trust issues were.

"But what if there comes a day that you wake up and figure out I'm too much work, too much trouble, and you wash your hands of me and walk away?" she said.

He slid his hand around her lower back, pulling her closer. "I'm holding on to you. You know I won't put up with your bullshit. Have you ever seen me walk away from anything that was too much work?"

She said nothing for a second, and he knew she was digging for something. "There is always a first, Garrett."

Worry. There it was, and he figured it would always be there.

"Have a little faith, Trinity. I know it goes against everything in you, but if I have to keep telling you every day for the rest of my life, I will, if that's what it will take."

She shut her eyes, fighting against what she wanted. "Can we just live together?"

He shook his head. "Nope. Marriage."

"But what about my parents, my family?"

"What about them? I'll talk to them."

"They'll never understand why I did what I did."

He wondered if even she understood. "I'll make them understand," he said, and when she didn't pull away, he continued. "So I'll give you two choices. Either we get married in front of Judge Peters on the day we get down off this mountain, or we do it on New Year's Eve, a small wedding, with just family."

There it was, the panic. "I can't get married that quickly, Garrett. There're plans, and dresses, and food. How about August?"

He just shook his head, leaned in, and pressed a kiss to her lips. He kissed her deeply and pulled back only when she softened against him. "Nope. New Year's Eve it is, I guess."

Her hands were fisted in his shirt. "My dad's going to kill you," she breathed out.

"Maybe so, but considering we're getting married and there's a baby, and I'm bringing you home, I figure I've earned a way back into his good graces."

"You're pretty cocky and sure of yourself."

He swayed with her, taking in the rumpled bed. "Yeah, and I'm sure you wouldn't have it any other way."

Then he leaned in again and kissed her deeply, tenderly, before laying her on the bed, hearing the wind howl outside, the winter storm around them, his baby sleeping soundly, and the woman who would be his wife under him.

CHAPTER
Eleven

Trinity slipped from bed when Skye stirred in the night, pulling a blanket over her naked body. Garrett too had stepped out into the cold cabin to shove more wood in the fire and heat the bottle on the stove. As he fed the baby, all she could think of was how he made her feel with every touch, every kiss, how he had loved her as he slipped inside her.

It had been different from the night that had created Skye, and it had touched something in her that she'd never let anyone get close to. There was something about the way he took his time loving her, tenderly. She could feel his strength around her, and she sensed that he would really make sure she and Skye had everything they needed.

He wouldn't walk away.

Now, as she lay in the circle of his arms again under the duvet, Skye once again fast asleep, she understood he really meant what he'd said.

"I can feel you thinking." His voice was deep and rumbled against her, unsettling her, making her feel things she'd never allowed herself to feel. Having all that male hardness pressed up to her, skin to skin, she remembered too well the moment he pulled off every stitch of her clothing and kissed her and touched her everywhere. For the first time, she had felt as if she truly belonged to someone.

"Aren't you ever afraid?" she said.

His hand pressed against her softly rounded belly, and he held her against him as he kissed her shoulder, his other hand skimming her leg. His hands were rough, and she couldn't have explained to anyone how good they felt.

"No, fear is just a placeholder for something else. Most times, fear means there's something you don't want to face, and being a cop, I can't afford to have that. I keep my head screwed on straight and see things as they are before I walk in."

She turned in his arms, seeing him in the dim light, her hands resting on his chest. She felt the hair, the pecs, his strength, his sureness, and she wondered about the second he'd realize his mistake. "That's crazy, Garrett. Everyone is scared. I'm scared."

He pressed a kiss to her forehead, his hand around the back of her neck. "I know you are, which is why it makes absolutely no sense that you moved into the middle of nowhere. There is facing your fears, and then there's hiding. We've already talked about this. Just give it some time, Trinity. I won't let anything happen to you."

She said nothing again as his hand slid lower, running over her skin. He had somehow maneuvered her on her back and was kissing her again, settling between her legs, when she heard something.

Garrett must have, as well, as he pulled back. She thought she heard voices, then a chainsaw and the rattle of the door before someone pounded on it.

"Trinity! Garrett!"

Shit! It was her dad.

Garrett was out of bed, pulling on his pants, and she pulled up the blankets, feeling more naked, if that was possible, as she jumped from bed and reached for the blue and white fluffy housecoat on a hook by the closet. She pulled it on just as Garrett strode out of the bedroom, buttoning his shirt.

The front door flew open, and she heard her dad's voice. She hurried out of the bedroom and pulled the door closed, but not before taking in the crib with her daughter, who was still sleeping.

She pushed back her hair. Logan stood in the doorway in a heavy winter coat and toque, with snow up to his knees. She could hear a chainsaw running outside.

"Hey, Merry Christmas!" he said. "Come here, you. What do you think you're doing, worrying your mom and me the way you did? It's been too long."

She found herself walking over to her dad and hugging him. He kissed the top of her head, and when she stepped back, she took in the way Garrett was watching her, his shirt buttoned but untucked.

She didn't think her dad had a clue of where he'd slept, though.

"So who's here with you? How're the roads?" Garrett said.

Trinity stood there, not daring to look back at the bedroom door.

"My brothers Joe and Ben are outside, taking apart that tree. You're lucky it didn't come down on this place—and the roads are not good, but we made it up here. Power's out all the way into town, too. But we'll have you out in no time. Your mom is looking forward to seeing you. Everyone is."

She didn't miss her dad's smile, but just then, the baby started crying. Her stomach pitched again and dropped to her knees as her dad stared at her and then lifted his gaze past her to the door. He said nothing as he slowly dragged it over to Garrett, who was giving everything to her.

"You want to get the baby, or do you want me to do it?" Garrett said.

Trinity took in her dad's confusion.

"Baby, what baby?" Logan said, dragging his gaze from her to Garrett and back. "What's going on here, Trinity?"

Here it was, the moment she'd avoided for so long. She opened her mouth to explain when Garrett said, "Our baby. You see, long story, and I will explain it, but suffice to say, Trinity and I had a baby, and we're getting married on New Year's Eve."

Her dad gave Garrett a glare filled with shock, surprise, the kind she didn't think she'd seen before in his face. As the seconds ticked by, the baby really started fussing, and she was forced to step into the bedroom. Skye's tiny fists were waving.

Trinity could hear her dad's voice and Garrett's, and she didn't have a clue what they were saying as she lifted Skye from the crib with the blanket and stepped back, barefoot, across the cold floor and into the living room.

Both her dad and Garrett looked her way. She wasn't sure what had passed between the two men, but Logan's entire expression changed as he walked toward her, taking in the baby. Then he slid his cold, rough hand under her chin and made her look up at him.

"You should have told us, Trinity. You okay?" he said, and he held his arms out and took Skye.

Garrett walked behind her and rested both hands on her shoulders. It was a support she'd never expected, and she found herself reaching back and gripping his hand. "She is now, and she's going to be okay. I'll make sure of it," he said.

"Well, right now, let's get you and the baby out of here and down this mountain," Logan said. "Garrett, seems you and I will need to settle some things between us."

As she looked up at Garrett, he nodded and inclined his head. She expected for him to be scared, but instead, all he seemed to ooze was confidence.

"And, Trinity, get dressed," Logan said. "If I were you, I'd figure out how you're going to explain to your mother why you kept your baby a secret." Then he slid Skye back into her arms.

Garrett slid one arm around her chest, holding her to him. She couldn't explain what it felt like as she took in her dad, his stern gaze, and how he was trying to make sense of this.

"I'm sorry, Dad. It seemed I didn't know how to tell anyone, and then I just didn't, and then it became easier to just hide…" She was leaning against Garrett and looked up at him, seeing the way he was watching her, confident, strong, taking in all of this. "I never told Garrett. He just found out."

Her dad froze her in his gaze, that long intense look.

"Just Dawn," she continued. "I planned to tell you and Mom, or I kept telling myself I would, but at the same time, it was easier to just stay up here and avoid it. It seems I've always done that, because I'm too scared of the unknown. I get it in my head that you and everyone will be disappointed or that something could be worse, even though it doesn't make sense now as I say it."

It was the first time she'd spoken those words, the first time her dad looked at her as if he really under-stood what she was saying. Then he reached over and touched the side of her head.

"I won't let anything happen to her," Garrett said.

Logan glanced at him, then dropped his gaze back to her again. "I'll hold you to that, Garrett," he said. "Now let's get out of here."

G arrett had expected Logan to give him the third degree, maybe even sit him down and threaten him within an inch of his life. What he hadn't expected was silence. Then there was the thought of Lori, the girl who had wanted more from him, which he hadn't been ready to give, yet here he was now, marrying someone else.

"So, tonight, is it?" said Jordy, another deputy. He had been in the department even before Logan. His dark hair was threaded with gray, and he knew everything about everyone. "The wedding, the last of your freedom. Could've thrown you a bachelor party… Still could!"

Logan appeared in the doorway of his office and jabbed a finger at Garrett. "Garrett, come in here," was all he said.

Garrett looked over at Jordy, who of course had noticed that Logan had been kind of cold with him.

"Sure," he replied, then strode across the bullpen, digging into each step.

In the sheriff's office, Logan walked around his desk but didn't sit down. He was in faded blue jeans, his hat on the coat hook in the corner, wearing the tan shirt they all wore. "Close the door," he said and gestured toward it. His hair was still thick, though mostly gray now. He settled his large hands on his hips, over his gun belt, which he always wore.

Garrett did just that and waited for what was coming, but Logan said nothing for a few more seconds.

Finally, he spoke. "You know, there are very few people who surprise me, Garrett. You hooked up with my daughter and knocked her up, and there was never even a mention of the two of you. I've had to take a few days to wrap my head around what happened. Do you have any idea what her mother and I have been through? We can't understand how she could have kept Skye a secret. It makes no sense. Even when I sat her down and talked to her, she clammed up tighter than I've ever seen her do. When Trinity doesn't want to talk, there's nothing you can do to make her."

He took in Logan, knowing well the last few days had been a shock. Trinity and Skye were now living with him in his small house at the edge of town. Her parents came by, and her sister, but no one had asked any hard questions, considering he'd been there every time they'd knocked on the door.

"She's a tough cookie, I know that," Garrett

said. "She has her reasons, and to Trinity, they were valid. If you're about to lecture me on what happened, you're too late. It shouldn't have happened, it was one of those things, but at the same time, I wouldn't change anything. I have a daughter now."

Logan stared back at him hard. He thought his boss was about to lay into him as he rested his hands on the desk and leaned down, looking at him as if he were about to rip a strip off him, as if he were a wet-behind-the-ears teenager.

"No disrespect, sir," Garrett continued, "but Trinity has never faced anything directly, so what she did doesn't surprise me." He stood his ground, his arms crossed.

Then he heard a voice outside that sounded like Lori. Shit, could this get any worse?

"You have all your ducks in a row?" Logan said. "Because if you marry my daughter, you had better make sure she's looked after. You may be my deputy, but I will seriously hurt you if she isn't happy."

He understood exactly what his boss was saying. "She will be, but I won't coddle her. That's all everyone has ever done. If you don't mind me saying, Sheriff, for so long, everyone has made things easier for her, not holding her accountable. I won't do that."

Logan glanced away. "So you're saying her mother and I are responsible for this, for her hiding up at a cabin in the middle of nowhere, keeping her baby a secret, as if she was terrified to tell us? It makes no sense. That makes no sense." He glanced over to him, and for a second, Garrett had the sense he'd overstepped.

"What I'm saying is we all remember what happened to her as a girl and what it did to her. She was never the same. At the same time, everyone seemed to go easier on her, and Trinity knew it. The only thing she knows is how to get her own way, and then, when something happens, she doesn't deal with it because she's afraid to make a choice."

"And you know how to handle her," Logan said. It wasn't a question.

Garrett wondered how much Logan had picked up over the last few days, watching Trinity and him. He was bossy, direct, and he didn't give in to any of the shenanigans that seemed to make up who she was.

"I do. I'll be good to her and my daughter. I am marrying her tonight," he stated.

Would Logan say anything otherwise? He gestured toward the door with his chin. "Well, then you'd better get out of here and get yourself ready—and make sure you take care of that other situation out there."

So he knew Lori was outside. Of course he did.

"I will," was all Garrett said before he pulled open the door.

He took in Lori, tall, slender, pretty, with short brown hair…but she wasn't Trinity. Her eyes were blue. She had been talking with Jordy, but she now turned, giving everything to him.

"Hey, Lori. I left you a few messages," he said. He

wondered if Logan was standing behind him as he strode into the bullpen.

Jordy must have known, as he made a face and stood up from where he leaned against the desk. "Well, I'll go clean some things up in back…" he said.

Logan followed him, leaving Garrett alone with a woman he had been so close and intimate with. He had ended things in a way that had him wanting to apologize, to somehow make this situation better.

"I suppose you heard that I'm getting married," he said. In that moment, the tension was so thick he could have cut it with a knife.

"I heard," she said. "It's amazing, how long we were together, and I couldn't get you to commit to me. You said, if I remember correctly, that you don't want a serious relationship. You just wanted something casual. Even when you said you wanted a break, I kind of thought, okay, I'd give you space, and then we'd figure it out. But then, finding out you have a baby and you're suddenly getting married, what am I to think?"

He could tell by the way she spoke that she was angry, hurt. She had every right to be.

"So it was me," she said. "Heard that Trinity hid up there at that cottage, hiding the baby from everyone, and she never would've told anyone about it. You sure it's yours? You know she has a reputation."

What was he supposed to say to her that would make this better? He dragged his hand over his neck and then gave her everything, knowing he needed to choose his words carefully. A woman scorned wasn't

good for his health. At the same time, he wasn't stepping into town gossip.

"It's mine, she's mine," he said. "I won't discuss
Trinity with you. I am marrying her tonight, but I
wanted to apologize to you, because even though I
don't love you, I do care."

She reached out and tried to hug him, but he held
her at arm's length.

"No, Lori, don't. This isn't okay."

"Garrett, please…a baby is fine. We can work it out.
We've been together a long time. Give me a chance,
give us a chance. I can make you happy. Trinity is…"

"Going to be my wife, Lori," he said. "I'm sorry,
so sorry, but I love her. There is no us. I enjoyed what
we had, but that was all it was. I'm sorry I hurt you
and that this happened."

She pulled her arms away. She was hurt. It was in
her face, the way she stepped back and then ran her
hand over her hair. And she was embarrassed. He
wished he could say something to make it better.

"Well, I guess I wish you all the best, then," she
said, and she stepped away. But she stopped after a
few feet and turned back to him, taking him in. She
really was pretty, nice, kind, but she didn't take his
breath away. "I hope Trinity will get it together, but
she's always been a mess, so I guess I wish you good
luck, and maybe when she breaks your heart, I won't
have to say I told you so. But I'll be waiting."

What was it about women? They could have a
mean streak.

"Good night, Lori," he said. "I think you know I'm a man of my word, so I won't be calling. I'm marrying Trinity, she'll be my wife, and I won't be looking elsewhere. Don't wait. You need to get on with your life. Go find yourself a guy who will love you the way you love him, because that's not me and never will be."

She seemed to consider something, then shook her head before walking out of the precinct, and he blew out a breath.

When he turned, Logan was standing there in the shadows, watching him, his brows raised.

"So you heard," he said.

Logan walked in and shrugged. "Couldn't help it. You thought it would be easy?" He stopped in front of him and crossed his arms.

Garrett shook his head. "No, I didn't, but at the same time, I hope she understood. I was clear that there's no future, but I can see now she was still hoping."

Logan just shrugged and then shook his head. "You told her, you were clear. That's all you can do. So how about we clear out here so you can get changed and go talk to Trinity?"

Before he could answer, his cell phone rang, and he pulled it out and saw Dawn's name. "Hey, we're just leaving…" he started.

"Well, that's good, because we've got a problem," Dawn said. "Trinity has locked herself in the back room of the church and won't open the door. She says she's changed her mind and the wedding is off and to let everyone know."

He lifted his head and gazed at the ceiling, not missing the confusion in Logan's expression. "Okay, we'll be right there," he replied, then hung up the phone and pocketed it before reaching for his coat on the back of his chair. "Trinity's freaking out," he said. "Need to go to the church. I'll meet you there."

He started out of the office and wondered if Logan had anticipated this. He hadn't, but he knew he should have—and as he glanced back, he was positive Logan was laughing.

Evidently, the man knew something he didn't.

CHAPTER
Thirteen

"Okay, everyone is waiting in the chapel, wondering what's going on and why you're taking so long," Dawn said. "Trinity, come on, open the door. This is just nerves. You can't seriously call off the wedding…"

Her sister could really carry on with the way she knocked on the old door. It rattled as Trinity took in her image in the small oval mirror, wearing the white lace wedding dress she had purchased off the rack just two days earlier from the small boutique by her mom's café.

Of course, she looked great, even taking into account how big her eyes were and the fact that she felt as if she was about to puke, all because she was supposed to be marrying Garrett Franke. Why the hell was she freaking out?

The pounding continued.

"Trinity, open this door right now and let me in!

You've ignored Mom and me. You can't hide in there all day."

She just turned to the locked door, still unable to believe she'd flicked the deadbolt. Garrett's voice rang through her mind as she stood there, feeling as if her life was careening like a runaway train, an impending disaster, and she didn't have a clue what to do or how to stop it. She was, as Garrett had put it so aptly, her own worst enemy. Like, what the hell was wrong with her?

As she stared at the door, her sister continued to pound and knock and rattle the knob.

She knew she was once again pushing Garrett away.

Then there were voices—male, she thought, right before there was a click and the door popped open. A few seconds later and there were Garrett and her sister, and she could hear Skye fussing outside as well. She knew her mom had her baby and was looking after her.

All she could do was stare in horror at Garrett, still dressed in his uniform, handing what looked like two bobby pins back to her sister.

"Seriously, Trinity, what the hell is going on with you...?" Dawn said as she stepped around Garrett, dressed in a hot pink dress, sleeves off the shoulders and straight to her knees. It was surprisingly flattering. Garrett reached for her arm and pulled her back, gesturing to the door with his head.

"Give us a second, Dawn," was all he said, and

she watched as he somehow maneuvered her out the door and then shut it, one hand on the knob, one on his gun belt.

All she could do was stare at his back and all that strength. How was it that a man could look so good from behind? There was something about a man in uniform, but Garrett took it to a whole other level. Then she realized he had turned and was looking right at her, and she wasn't sure what his expression was. He seemed to be considering something, pissed, angry, or so done with her. Maybe all of the above.

He glanced away, and she wondered what he was thinking. Then he leveled everything on her and took a step closer to her. His footsteps were heavy, and she just stood there like an idiot.

"What's going on this time, Trinity?" he said. The million-dollar question. "Dawn called, freaking out, saying you had called the wedding off and said to send everyone home, and I find you locked in the back room here, hiding out." He raised a brow and took another step toward her. "Seems that's something you like to do—hide out, I mean. You have to stop this. The preacher is here, waiting, and your family is in the chapel, wondering what's up, so talk to me." He took another step and another until he was right in front of her and she was forced to lift her gaze and look up at him.

"It's a mistake is all, Garrett. We can't do this. You're marrying me only because of Skye. I told you that's not a reason to get married, and this is a mistake. I feel it so deeply. I know you'll wake up one day and walk out the door, wondering what you were thinking, and then it will be ugly between us. So let's just skip the wedding…"

He was shaking his head again. "No, I told you before that we're getting married. We've already been through this. We have a baby, and we're getting married. You're not giving me enough credit if you think I'm so shallow that I'd marry you and then walk away. You think I don't know you're terrified? I can see everything you hide from everyone, including yourself."

She pulled her arms across her middle. "I'm not scared, Garrett. I'm being realistic and have come to my senses. You should, too."

This time he laughed and shook his head. "Bullshit, Trinity. You're terrified. And when you're scared you run and push everyone away. I told you this stops now." He was so damn bossy and arrogant and confident, and she'd kill for just a little of that. "Hey, over here!" He actually snapped his fingers, and she lowered her hands, fisting them, wondering how much it would take to push him out the door.

"I'm not a dog," she snapped. "Don't treat me like one."

His amber eyes flashed, and she knew it wasn't humor. He was a man who meant business. "I know very well who you are, Trinity, and you're being over-dramatic again. Of course you're not a dog. You're the mother of my daughter, the woman I'm going to marry and spend my life with, but at the same time, I'm not sitting back and letting you spin out of control. You pull into yourself, and that's exactly what you just did a second ago. You've done it for so long, and as soon as you do, this is what happens. So, again, what the hell are you so scared of? Tell me something reasonable. Talk to me. It's just you and me here."

She shut her eyes for a second and felt his hand on her cheek, her shoulder. He was so close that she could feel his heat, his strength, his confidence. There was something about him. She didn't think he ever questioned anything he did. "You won't understand," she said, "because I can't even explain it to myself, this feeling I have when I think of you and me. You're so charismatic, charming, strong."

He gave her everything in that one look. "And that's a bad thing?"

"Too confident," she said, and then what did he do but touch the side of her face, her hair? "And I'm not. I'm trying not to be scared. You're right about that."

"Then I'll be confident for both of us. Trust me, here."

He just kept saying all the right things.

"You're too good looking. You'll wake up and realize your mistake, and—"

"You're not giving me enough credit, Trinity. You know I'm a man of my word."

She did, but she didn't want him this way. He'd resent her. She was sure of it.

"Maybe that's the problem," she said. "I don't want to be an obligation, or for Skye to have that held over her, that you married me because of her."

He said nothing, and for a second she expected him to walk out of there and agree. "You're still pushing, but the thing is, I'm not walking," he said. "I'm not going anywhere, and we've already decided, Trinity. You start overthinking and creating a problem that isn't there." He was still touching her, and she had to fight the need to step back, away from a man she could feel herself wanting to sink into. "You're scared, terrified. What is it, Trinity? Come on, tell me."

"You want the real reason?" she said, wondering if he'd laugh.

"Please, come on…" Both his hands rested on her shoulders and slid down, caressing her arms. He didn't step back, didn't pull away. He just held her there, making her feel so safe.

"Because I'm in love with you, Garrett. Maybe I've always been in love with you."

He appeared confused and angled his head. "And that's a problem how?"

"Because I'm afraid you won't love me the way I love you, and you'll walk out the door because I'm too much work—as you've said, a pain in the ass."

Garrett stepped closer, settled both his hands over her cheeks, and really looked at her. "Trinity, Trinity, what am I going to do with you?" He leaned in and pressed a kiss to her lips, letting it linger just a bit before pulling back. "You're right that you're a challenge, and difficult, but I know well what I'm walking into with you. You don't know how to make anything easy, and you worry about things others don't give a passing thought to. You're a pain in the ass at times, but you're my pain in the ass. Everything difficult, every frustrating thing you do, and all the bumps in the road you continue to drive over because you don't understand what easy is…well, I will gladly take them on, because I'll get you."

It took her a second to understand what he was saying.

"I loved you long ago," he said. "I just wouldn't admit it to anyone, mainly myself. When I saw you and our baby, I knew there was no way I was letting you go. I'd do whatever it took to get a ring on your finger, get you under my roof, in my bed, building a life with me. I have no doubt you'll make every day as difficult as possible. You don't simply take the status quo. You're headstrong, and I have no doubt you're not easily pleased, but I'll enjoy every moment of handling you. You're a challenge, Trinity, a welcome one. I don't want easy. If I did, we wouldn't be standing here, discussing this."

"That doesn't sound like a compliment," she replied. She couldn't resist letting him pull her closer into his arms, pressing her hands over his chest, feeling his badge pinned there. The uneasiness that had plagued her moments ago dissipated a bit.

His gaze dipped to her lips, and she waited for him to lean in and kiss her again. "Well, as I said, I seem to enjoy your difficulty. In case you didn't notice, Trinity, the only woman I have eyes for is you. So, any other worries, or can we now get married?"

"You need to get changed," she said.

This time he did smile, the kind of smile that rocked her and had her stomach pounding with butterflies as he slowly shook his head. "No, I think not. We're getting married as is, right now. You think I'm going to give you any more time to start freaking out again?" He held out his arm and lifted a brow.

"But what about my dad?" she said, setting her hand on his arm.

He rested his hand over hers, holding her in place. "Oh, I suspect he's standing at the front of the church with the rest of your family, waiting for me to walk you in."

"This isn't the way we're supposed to do this," she added as he started walking her to the door, then stopped, holding her beside him as he looked down at her.

"There's no rulebook, Trinity, on how this goes down. The only thing that matters is me getting you to the altar one way or another."

Then he had her out the door and down the aisle, and she took in her parents, her baby, Scott and Dawn, and her uncles and their wives lingering at the front of the church.

Everyone took a seat, the preacher took his place, and Trinity didn't pull her gaze from the hottie deputy who stood before her, said "I do," and slipped a plain gold band on her finger.

"For better or worse, I'm not letting you go," he

said, and then he leaned in and kissed her as she heard her baby cry and her family cheer.

For the first time, as Garrett pulled back but didn't let her go, Trinity really believed that he meant every word of what he'd said.

This really was going to be a wonderful life.

Turn the page for a sneak peek of
THE FAMILY SECRET in THE O'CONNELLS
Available in print, eBook & Audio

"This was a very explosive and heart wrenching story. A body is found and the DA is out for blood. As long as it's O'Connell blood, he doesn't much care whose."

KEC200

"This is a tale that is sure to keep you riveted from start to finish. It has twists upon twists, and as the plot thickens, you'll find the mystery only deepens."

CATLOU

"Wow what drama, what tension, what suspense."

SUSAN JORDENS

About the O'Connells

The O'Connells of Livingston, Montana, are not your typical family. Follow them on their journey to the dark and dangerous side of love in a series of romantic thrillers you won't want to miss. Raised by a single mother after their father's mysterious disappearance eighteen years ago, the six grown siblings live in a small town with all kinds of hidden secrets, lies, and deception. Much like the contemporary family romance series focusing on the Friessens, this romantic suspense series follows the lives of the O'Connell family as each of the siblings searches for love.

The O'Connells

The Neighbor
The Third Call
The Secret Husband
The Quiet Day

The Commitment, An O'Connell Novella
The Missing Father
The Hometown Hero
Justice
The Family Secret
The Fallen O'Connell
The Return of the O'Connells
And The She Was Gone
The Stalker
The O'Connell Family Christmas
The Girl Next Door
Broken Promises
The Gatekeeper

Raymond O'Connell was the love of Iris's life —from the day she met him, to the day a year later when she married him, to the tragic night before she never saw him again.

Some would say they had the perfect all-American life. Now, eighteen years later, questions arise about the night her husband disappeared, leaving a bloody knife and a letter addressed to her, in which he said goodbye and told her not to look for him, with not even a second thought for her and their six children.

The scandal when Raymond left rocked the community, fueling widespread rumors, from him running away with his mistress to him being dead. But through it all, Iris kept her head down, keeping the secret of what really happened. Although her children often wondered, and her eldest thought he was protecting her from something heinous when she asked him to get rid of the knife, what they didn't know was that their father wasn't who they thought he was. Making sure his secret didn't come out was the only way to keep her family together.

Now, Iris can no longer keep her life with Raymond O'Connell buried, because her adult children are asking questions. The only thing she can think to do to protect herself and them is to enlist the help of a lawyer, her daughter's husband, fearing that once the truth starts to surface, it could change everything about their lives.

The secret of their father, which Iris has hidden for so long now, has the potential to destroy everything the O'Connells have built for themselves, and once the truth of who Raymond O'Connell really was comes out, it will put a target on all of them, and their lives in peaceful Livingston, Montana, will never be the same.

The Family Secret

CHAPTER 1

At one time, if anyone had tried to tell Iris she would end up with the stable life she had now, she'd have told them they were crazy. For so many years, she'd kept her head down, putting everything on hold for her children and pushing away that hurt, that ache, that pain that had shredded her heart, having to climb out of the dark pit that wanted to drag her down.

Now, as she pulled in a breath, she had to remind herself that she no longer felt that guttural ache that had stolen her peace of mind and distracted her from all those small things that should've put a smile on her face in her children's early years. She'd forgotten exactly when it had happened, when that wretched, visceral ache, which she'd screamed into a pillow to ease, had just left.

Her six children, whom she couldn't imagine a life without, were all grown now, and she still centered everything around them. Her life was theirs. At the same time, there were days she wondered whether she had permanently scarred them, whether she could've done better.

She took in the concrete buildings, the bustling streets, the restaurants and bars and stores, and the scent of the autumn day on the breeze. These people made Livingston her home. It was a part of who she was, though there were times she had to tell herself she wasn't a fraud.

The light of day seemed so different from the shadows of night. The darkness still called to her when she was alone, looking out into the yard. She wondered what was hiding there, what was waiting to tear down the façade she'd built and take away everything that put a smile on her face, all the reasons she could now hold her head high. It was just a feeling she couldn't shake, one that had suddenly reemerged the moment her children learned of the night she wished she could forget.

She lifted her hand in a wave at a couple she knew, then another neighbor, people she knew well had gossiped behind her back at one time after she went from being a married woman to a single mother, struggling alone with six kids. It had cut her to the quick. Yes, Raymond O'Connell had been there one day and gone the next, and the rumors about why had left her feeling more alone than anything.

Of course it still smarted, if she really thought about it now. How did one go about shaking off all those hurtful rumors? People had trashed her character, saying she wasn't good enough, that she must've done something to deserve such a fate, that she was screwing up big-time when it came to her kids, all because the O'Connells no longer fit the all-American mold of how a family was supposed to be.

She clutched her bargain-bin purse, wearing a plain white T-shirt and loose red cardigan over slimming blue jeans. She didn't have to look in a mirror to know that while she was just Mom around her grown children, any man out there would've given her a second look. It was just who she was. Even though time hadn't been her friend, her lack of money while the kids were young had kept her from eating her way into a pity party. She was grateful for that, at least, considering being slim and attractive had been the furthest thing from her mind for too many years.

She took in the nightclub in front of her, where staff were serving the lunch crowd, then turned to the glass industrial door with the words "Karen O'Connell & Jack Curtis, Lawyers" etched in black. An office over a nightclub. She couldn't help the smile that tugged at her lips.

She was so proud of her daughter Karen, a lawyer, and Karen's husband, Jack, who had a charm and charisma about him that reminded her so much of her own husband. Maybe that was why she watched him from a distance, wondering when he'd turn into someone else. There was something about him that told her he was holding on to the kind of secrets he would never share with another person. How did she know? It was just one of those feelings she got about people she spent time with.

She knew there was so much more to his life and his secrets than she would ever know, but she also knew he'd do anything for her daughter.

Iris forced herself to touch the steel handle and pull open the door, feeling it scrape against the metal lip on the ground. She started up the steps, her shoes squeaking to announce her arrival. Her palms sweated, and her heart kicked up with each step. She made herself pull in a breath.

She could hear talking, a man's voice—Jack, she thought—as she stepped up on the landing, her hand on the rail, taking in the narrow hall and the open office door. The walls were dingy, nicked, and needed a fresh coat of paint.

She stepped into the reception area, seeing the door to Karen's office closed. Jack was sitting at the receptionist's desk, a position they still hadn't filled. He lifted his hand in a wave to her, the phone to his ear, his blue eyes mysterious and his dark hair neatly groomed. He already had a five o'clock shadow, and it was barely noon. He hung up the phone and stood.

"Iris, I didn't know you were coming by," he said, gesturing toward her and walking around the desk. "Karen is actually in court right now."

She shook her head, taking in his blue striped dress shirt and dark pants. He was attractive, and she wondered, looking at him now, what it was about him that gave her that sense of familiarity, reminding her of a man she'd once thought of dozens of times a day —a man who, thankfully, had now become just a passing thought.

"That's fine," Iris said. "I actually stopped by to see you. Do you have a minute?"

She wasn't sure what he was thinking. He hesitated, and a soft smile touched his lips as he leaned against the desk and crossed his arms, giving her everything with just a look. She glanced over her shoulder to the open door and then back to him.

"You know what?" he said. "Let's go talk in the office. Seems my wife and I can't decide on a new place. She likes this dump, and we end up having to share an office, or one of us works out in reception…" He opened the office door and walked in, then stepped aside so he could close it behind her.

He had evidently picked up on her unease and her need for privacy, even though she didn't have a clue what she was going to say. He gestured to the chairs in front of the desk, and she squeezed her purse over her shoulder.

"Please, Iris, have a seat," he said. "So you wanted to talk to me?"

She walked over to the chair and sat down, and she expected him to sit behind the desk across from her, but instead he sat beside her. Something in his blue eyes was so intense. He didn't look away, didn't pull away. He seemed amused, curious, but she wondered how curious he'd be when he learned the truth of what she'd done and who she really was.

There it was, silence, because she'd missed her cue to speak.

She slid her purse strap off her shoulder and took

her time setting it on the floor. When she looked up, he was still waiting patiently.

"Is everything all right, Iris?" he said, then glanced to the door and back to her. He leaned forward, his forearms resting on his knees, and she took in the scar along the side of his face, tiny, just barely there. He started to laugh and rubbed the back of his head. "Are you upset with me or something?"

She gestured toward him. "No, no, nothing like that. I just need a second to find the words or rip the bandage off, so to speak. You know, Karen doesn't know I've come here, and neither do my other children…" She hesitated.

Jack glanced to the door again and sat up straighter, an odd smile touching his lips. "Okay. You do know that whatever you say to me, I won't share it. It stays between us."

She reached for her purse and unzipped it, then opened up her wallet, seeing the bills inside. She pulled out a dollar bill and rested it on the desk, one hand pressed over it as she clutched her wallet in the other.

He inhaled and stared at her hand. Evidently, he had figured out this was something more than a friendly visit.

"I want to hire you as my lawyer, Jack," she said, then pushed the bill closer to him.

His expression had suddenly turned serious as he dragged his gaze over to her. His blue eyes were so different from the O'Connell blue. He hesitated, and all she did was lower her gaze to the money on the desk beside him, forcing a swallow past the lump in her throat and fighting the instinctual tremble in her hand.

"Is it true that as my lawyer, you can't share anything?" she said, though she knew it was, considering she'd listened to everything Karen had shared with her during her studies to become a lawyer—every law, all the rights, everything that could be used against someone.

Jack pulled in a breath, hesitating only a second before he settled his hand over the bill and held it up. "Okay, so this is a retainer?" He didn't laugh. He could obviously see that she had no intention of saying a word until he said what she needed to hear.

"Yes, consider me your lawyer," he said, then shoved the dollar bill in his pocket. He stood up and walked around the desk, changing from her daughter's husband to a businessman. Maybe he needed to have something between them to ensure a level of professionality.

She did, too, but more for courage, because she couldn't remember feeling the kind of fear she was feeling right now. She wondered whether he could hear her relief as she breathed out.

"So you're looking for a will or something done up?" he said. The way he asked, it sounded as if he couldn't imagine anything else. He actually reached for a legal pad in one of Karen's drawers and rummaged for a pen as Iris silently wished it were that simple.

"I married a man and had six of his children only

to learn he wasn't the man I thought he was," she said. "The night he left, I did something."

Jack leaned on the desk, ready to write, and froze, pen in hand. He slowly dragged his gaze up and over to her, and she had to force herself to continue before the fear that was threatening to choke her took over and shut down her voice. Her throat was thick, and she cleared it.

"I'm afraid that one day very soon, there will be a knock on my door, a reckoning for what I did and what I know. In fact, I can already feel it, something coming, whispering that my time is up."

She'd expected shock, maybe outrage, not the stillness that was staring back at her. He opened his mouth to say something, but instead he simply stood up, walked over to the door, and locked it.

When he turned, she could see he needed a minute to get his head around the bomb she'd just dropped. He started back to the desk, digging into each step, but instead of sitting, he rested his hands on the back of the chair right beside her and leaned down. His gaze was imploring, intense, and she knew she had all his attention.

"Okay, I think you'd better start at the beginning," he said, "and don't leave anything out."

The Family Secret

CHAPTER 2

Jack needed a second.

He stared at Iris, whose face was so much like his wife's. Her chest rose as she waited for him to say something, as if waiting for the other shoe to drop. The blue of her eyes resembled his wife's in some ways, but where Karen's cheeks were plump, Iris had a narrow face and nose, and her lips were not quite as full.

He realized that what she'd just said concerned something he'd always seen as a big black circle of mystery about his wife's father, just something none of the O'Connells spoke of.

Jack stood up and dragged his hand over his face, hearing the scrape of whiskers. Iris pressed her lips together, and he found himself looking to the door and hesitating, wondering when Karen would be done with her motion at the courthouse and back. It could be hours or minutes.

"I'm not sure where to start," Iris finally said.

It wasn't as if Jack had trouble getting clients to talk, but everyone was different, and this was Iris O'Connell, his wife's mother, his family. "Well, let's start with the fact that you're here to see me. I need to ask, does Karen know about whatever this is?"

She hesitated and glanced away. "Not everything, only the part that Owen knew. My son came downstairs just as I had wrapped up the knife in some cloth. The office was a mess, broken things, paper everywhere, and there was blood. I asked Owen to get rid of the knife. I never really considered what he thought, because he never said anything. But apparently, he buried it in the woods. This just came out now. Someone saw him do it, that lady who was part of the recent high school trouble. I know Owen and Marcus have taken care of it now. They got the knife back. That woman had something on us, something that would prompt questions I don't want to answer. I didn't realize what Owen thought I had done until he and Marcus came to me. Suzanne was there, and Luke was home, too. They don't know that I know this, but they shared it with Ryan and Karen even though I asked them not to… But they don't know everything." Her knuckles were white from gripping her purse.

"How is it possible that I believed someone I was so close and intimate with, then learned that everything was a lie? I told Owen that I needed his help to keep us together. Like, what the fuck is wrong with me? Owen was just a kid, a teenager. He went from just a typical sixteen-year-old to a father figure overnight, having to watch over his siblings. I knew it, but I was drowning in everything, trying to figure out how to put one foot in front of the other." She sighed.

He realized he'd never had this kind of trouble before with a client, worrying about whether they had done the worst thing imaginable. Often, they had, but in this case, he wasn't sure he wanted to know. What the hell was he going to tell Karen?

Nothing.

"So there was a knife and blood and a crime scene, and you basically…"

"Cleaned up," she said. "I think that's what you're getting at. Yes, Jack, I cleaned up a crime scene. I cleaned up the office, I destroyed evidence, I dragged my impressionable teenage son into something unknowingly because he walked into the middle of everything as I was trying to wrap my head around it. You know what? That night has been with me for so long, yet there I was, all these years later, thinking it had finally stopped haunting me. I had spent night after night trying to make sense of what happened."

She killed him, he thought. It was his first thought, yet he couldn't ask. "Go on," he said. "Tell me everything, Iris, so I can figure out how to help."

She merely nodded. He could see how shallow her breathing was. This wasn't the Iris O'Connell he was used to, who was always smiling and laughing with her kids. "Raymond had been acting strangely for some time, and I suspected he was involved in something, but I kept telling myself it was nothing. Have you ever known someone so well and then realized one day that you didn't know anything about them? I did."

She didn't let him answer. He could see how she was struggling to find the words. "I just told myself I likely didn't want to know, or it was nothing. Men I'd never seen before had started showing up late, when the kids were in bed, when I was getting ready to turn in for the night and expecting Raymond to follow. He'd started keeping to his office downstairs. When I came home with the kids to make dinner, there were times I found him there instead of at work. He was good with his hands, could fix anything. But he became dismissive, secretive, and I could feel him pushing me away. Then that night happened…"

That was all she said. Then she coughed.

"Let me get you some water," Jack said, striding over to the small bar fridge. He opened it and reached for one of the bottles his wife kept stocked for him, then closed the fridge and took a second before turning around. Held out the water to her.

"Thank you." She unscrewed the cap and took a swallow.

Jack took in the legal pad waiting on the desk for him to write something. His wife's mother was confessing to something she'd done, and right now, he was positive this knowledge would be just something else that could come between him and his wife.

"So let's go back to that night," he said. "You said there were men there. Who were these men?"

She pulled in a breath and glanced down. "You

know, Jack, I don't know who they were. I'd never seen them before. I'd only heard voices and gone down once, and I saw a man, balding, sitting with my husband. The other standing. I'd never seen him before. But have you ever met someone and realized there was something about them, something that made you swear you'd never forget their face? Well, there was something about them that bothered me.

"That was the first time Raymond ever dismissed me—you know, telling me to go to bed, that he had business that didn't concern me. I wanted to stand my ground and tell him where to go, but the way he looked at me and the amusement on the stranger's face… I left. Of course, I waited for him, but I eventually fell asleep. I'm not even sure he came to bed. I was furious, and you know what I did? I ate that anger. I didn't speak. Then I realized after days that he wasn't going to apologize. That was the first time that it seemed as if he'd suddenly changed into a different person. He was no longer the tall, dashing, dark-haired, blue-eyed devil who'd arrived in town one day and swept me off my feet, a man who'd turned my life, our life, into a dream. It had turned into a nightmare."

He was pacing now, his arms across his chest. "I'm not understanding what happened. You need to tell me what you did. Did you hurt him?"

She made a face and started to say something, but she pulled in a breath, and her jaw slackened. She glanced over to the window and shook her head before looking back to him. "There was a letter on his desk, in his handwriting. All it said was 'Goodbye. Don't look for me. I'm sorry.' The problem is, Jack, I had woken up on the floor of his office and seen the mess and the blood, and I didn't remember what had happened or how I'd got there. All I knew was that I was suddenly standing in the middle of something gruesome, bloody, and I had no idea where my husband was…"

He was positive there was more. He stared at her as she lowered her head, looking down at her hands, flexing them and holding her ringless fingers out in front of her as if they held all the answers.

"Are you telling me you woke up in a crime scene, and there was blood, a knife, and a messy room, and you don't know how you got there? You remember nothing? Were you knocked out? You didn't call the police?"

She shook her head, and for a minute, he had to remind himself this was Karen's mother, because if it had been anyone else, he'd have told them he didn't believe them.

"I don't understand why you didn't call the police, the sheriff," he said. "That makes absolutely no sense, Iris."

"You don't get it, Jack?" she said.

He just stared at her, because none of this made any sense. "No. Fill me in, Iris, because from where I'm sitting, you haven't given me one reason yet why you couldn't have called the police. Why didn't you report him missing? People had to wonder where he was. He had a job, right?"

All Iris did was lift her blue eyes to him, and this time her expression was filled with a confidence he wasn't entirely comfortable with. "Reporting him missing wasn't an option," she said, "because when I woke up, the knife was in my hand."

"Lorhainne Eckhart is one of my go to authors when I want a guaranteed good book. So many twists and turns, but also so much love and such a strong sense of family."

(LORA W., REVIEWER)

New York Times & USA Today bestseller Lorhainne Eckhart is best known for writing Raw Relatable Real Romance where "Morals and family are running themes." As one fan calls her, she is the "Queen of the family saga." (aherman) writing "the ups and downs of what goes on within a family but also with some suspense, angst and of course a bit of romance thrown in for good measure." Follow Lorhainne on Bookbub to receive alerts on New Releases and Sales and join her mailing list at LorhainneEckhart.com for her Monday Blog, all book news, giveaways and FREE reads. With over 120 books, audiobooks, and multiple series published and available at all, retailers now translated into six languages. She is a multiple recipient of the Readers' Favorite Award for Suspense and Romance, and lives in the Pacific Northwest on an island, is the mother of three, her oldest has autism and she is an advocate for never giving up on your dreams.

"Lorhainne Eckhart has this uncanny way of just hitting the spot every time with her books."

(CAROLINE L., REVIEWER)

The O'Connells: *The O'Connells of Livingston, Montana are not your typical family. A riveting collection of stories surrounding the ups and downs of what goes on within a family but also with some suspense, angst and of course a bit of romance thrown in for good measure. "I thought I loved the Friessens, but I absolutely adore the O'Connell's. Each and every book has different genres of stories, but the one thing in common is how she is able to wrap it around the family, which is the heart of each story." (C. Logue)*

The Friessens: *An emotional big family romance series, the Friessen family siblings find their relationships tested, lay their hearts on the line, and discover lasting love! "Lorhainne Eckhart is one of my go to authors when I want a guar-*

anteed good book. So many twists and turns, but also so much love and such a strong sense of family." (Lora W., Reviewer)

The Parker Sisters: *The Parker Sisters are a close-knit family, and like any other family they have their ups and downs. Eckhart has crafted another intense family drama… "The character development is outstanding, and the emotional investment is high…" (Aherman, Reviewer)*

The McCabe Brothers: *Join the five McCabe siblings on their journeys to the dark and dangerous side of love! An intense, exhilarating collection of romantic thrillers you won't want to miss. — "Eckhart has a new series that is definitely worth the read. The queen of the family saga started this series with a spin-off of her wildly successful Friessen series." From a Readers' Favorite award —winning author and "queen of the family saga" (Aherman)*

Billy Jo McCabe Mystery: *The social worker and the cop, an unlikely couple drawn together on a small, secluded Pacific Northwest island where nothing is as it seems. Protecting the innocent comes*

at a cost, and what seems to be a sleepy,
quiet town is anything but.

*Lorhainne loves to hear from her readers! You can connect with
me at:*

www.LorhainneEckhart.com
lorhainneeckhart.le@gmail.com

Leave the Light On
In the Moment
In the Family
In the Silence
In the Charm
Unexpected Consequences
It Was Always You
The First Time I Saw You
Welcome to My Arms
Welcome to Boston
I'll Always Love You
Ground Rules
A Reason to Breathe
You Are My Everything
Anything For You
The Homecoming
Stay Away From My Daughter
The Bad Boy
A Place of Our Own
The Visitor
All About Devon
Long Past Dawn
How to Heal a Heart
Keep Me In Your Heart

The O'Connells
The Neighbor
The Third Call
The Secret Husband
The Quiet Day
The Commitment

The Missing Father
The Hometown Hero
Justice
The Family Secret
The Fallen O'Connell
The Return of the O'Connells
And The She Was Gone
The Stalker
The O'Connell Family Christmas
The Girl Next Door
Broken Promises
The Gatekeeper
The Hunted

The McCabe Brothers
Don't Stop Me (Vic)
Don't Catch Me (Chase)
Don't Run From Me (Aaron)
Don't Hide From Me (Luc)
Don't Leave Me (Claudia)
Out of Time

A Billy Jo McCabe Mystery
Nothing As it Seems
Hiding in Plain Sight
The Cold Case
The Trap
Above the Law
The Stranger at the Door
The Children
The Last Stand

The Charity

The Wilde Brothers
The One (Joe and Margaret)
The Honeymoon, A Wilde Brothers Short
Friendly Fire (Logan and Julia)
Not Quite Married, A Wilde Brothers Short
A Matter of Trust (Ben and Carrie)
The Reckoning, A Wilde Brothers Christmas
Traded (Jake)
Unforgiven (Samuel)
The Holiday Bride

Married in Montana
His Promise
Love's Promise
A Promise of Forever

The Parker Sisters
Thrill of the Chase
The Dating Game
Play Hard to Get
What We Can't Have
Go Your Own Way
A June Wedding

Kate & Walker
One Night
Edge of Night
Last Night

Walk the Right Road Series
The Choice
Lost and Found
Merkaba
Bounty
Blown Away: The Final Chapter
He Came Back

The Saved Series
Saved
Vanished
Captured

Single Titles
Loving Christine